*"Jess, what made you do that?
He thinks that you and I are—"*

"Serious," she said. "Isn't that what you wanted? Now he sees you as a man broaching marriage. At least, a relationship. You're dependable. Stable. All those good things."

"Thanks, but what do I do when you leave and don't come back?"

"Let's pretend, Derek. Take it one step at a time." She'd thought Derek would be pleased, but seeing his panic, she suspected she'd made a mistake. "I'm sorry, Derek. I was only trying to help."

"Don't be sorry." A mischievous smile brightened his face. "I love the idea the more I think of it. Sure. Why not pretend...?"

D0051612

Dear Reader,

We have some incredibly fun and romantic Silhouette Romance titles for you this July. But as excited as we are about them, we also want to hear from *you!* Drop us a note—or visit www.eHarlequin.com—and tell us which stories you enjoyed the most, and what you'd like to see from us in the future.

We know you love emotion-packed romances, so don't miss Cara Colter's CROWN AND GLORY cross-line series installment, *Her Royal Husband*. Jordan Ashbury had no idea the man who'd fathered her child was a prince—until she reported for duty at his palace! Carla Cassidy spins an enchanting yarn in *More Than Meets the Eye*, the first of our A TALE OF THE SEA, the must-read Silhouette Romance miniseries about four very special siblings.

The temperature's rising not just outdoors, but also in Susan Meier's *Married in the Morning*. If the ring on her finger and the Vegas hotel room were any clue, Gina Martin was now the wife of Gerrick Green! Then jump into Lilian Darcy's tender *Pregnant and Protected*, about a fiery heiress who falls for her bodyguard....

Rounding out the month, Gail Martin crafts a fun, lighthearted tale about two former high school enemies in *Let's Pretend...*. And we're especially delighted to welcome new author Betsy Eliot's *The Brain & the Beauty*, about a young mother who braves a grumpy recluse in his dark tower.

Happy reading—and please keep in touch!

Mary-Theresa Hussey

Mary-Theresa Hussey
Senior Editor

Please address questions and book requests to:
Silhouette Reader Service
U.S.: 3010 Walden Ave., P.O. Box 1325, Buffalo, NY 14269
Canadian: P.O. Box 609, Fort Erie, Ont. L2A 5X3

Let's Pretend...

GAIL MARTIN

SILHOUETTE *Romance*®

Published by Silhouette Books

America's Publisher of Contemporary Romance

If you purchased this book without a cover you should be aware
that this book is stolen property. It was reported as "unsold and
destroyed" to the publisher, and neither the author nor the
publisher has received any payment for this "stripped book."

With love to my longtime high school friends:
Shirley, Phyllis, Joyce and Joann,
who shared my growing pains and supported me
as a writer and friend through the years. Thank you.

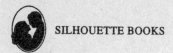 SILHOUETTE BOOKS

ISBN 0-373-19604-0

LET'S PRETEND...

Copyright © 2002 by Gail Gaymer Martin

All rights reserved. Except for use in any review, the reproduction
or utilization of this work in whole or in part in any form by any
electronic, mechanical or other means, now known or hereafter
invented, including xerography, photocopying and recording, or in
any information storage or retrieval system, is forbidden without
the written permission of the editorial office, Silhouette Books,
300 East 42nd Street, New York, NY 10017 U.S.A.

All characters in this book have no existence outside the imagination of
the author and have no relation whatsoever to anyone bearing the same
name or names. They are not even distantly inspired by any individual
known or unknown to the author, and all incidents are pure invention.

This edition published by arrangement with Harlequin Books S.A.

® and TM are trademarks of Harlequin Books S.A., used under license.
Trademarks indicated with ® are registered in the United States Patent
and Trademark Office, the Canadian Trade Marks Office and in other
countries.

Visit Silhouette at www.eHarlequin.com

Printed in U.S.A.

GAIL MARTIN

lives in front of her computer in Lathrup Village, Michigan, with her real-life hero, Bob. Growing up in nearby Madison Heights, Gail wrote poems and stories as a child. In her preteens, she progressed to Nancy Drew-type mysteries, teenage romances with a tragic ending. She had a lot to learn about romance.

Gail is multipublished in nonfiction and fiction with twelve novels, five novellas and many more to come. Her Steeple Hill Love Inspired novel *Upon a Midnight Clear* won a Holt Medallion in 2001. Besides writing, Gail enjoys singing, public speaking and presenting writers' workshops. She believes that laughter gets her through even the darkest moment.

She loves to hear from her readers. Write to her on the Internet at martinga@aol.com or at P.O. Box 760063, Lathrup Village, MI 48076.

Come one, come all to

Royal Oak High School's Centennial Celebration!

September 17

You won't want to miss old friends, teachers and even old flames...
But remember to leave those old high school grudges behind!

Hosted by Royal Oak's favorite roving reporter:

Derek Randolph

Chapter One

"Blast it!"

Peering past the useless windshield wipers into the heavy downpour, Jessamy Cosette felt the thud-thud of a flat tire. She'd driven 270 miles from Cincinnati without mishap, and in two more miles she'd reach her destination. Royal Oak. But her journey was like a dart game—hitting somewhere near the center wasn't the same as scoring a bull's-eye.

She edged to the freeway shoulder and smacked her fist on the steering wheel. Her images of the lovely Michigan Indian summer washed from her mind as quickly as golden red leaves drifted away on the wind. Storming dusk had settled across the sky, and the high walls of the freeway rose around her like a cement canyon. The only thing she could picture now was her drowned body floating down this aqueduct of highway…lost forever.

Since Meg Sullivan's call two weeks earlier, Jess had had second thoughts—then third and fourth. Coming home for the high school's centennial celebration and seeing her dearest high-school friend sounded wonderful, but staying in the same house with Meg's younger brother, Derek Randolph, weighed on her like a bad case of food poisoning.

Jess hadn't seen the hulking, obnoxious football player since she'd graduated from high school and he had been in the tenth grade. But he'd remained in her thoughts, her torment for years. If he called her "String Bean" or "Frenchie" again, she'd kill him.

Facing the dreadful possibility of murdering her best friend's brother, she stared at the vanishing taillights of one car after another flying past her like a Concorde along a runway. If anyone was going to change her tire, it looked as if it would have to be her. And since she'd never changed one in her life, she was faced with that horrible reality, too.

As she stared into the relentless downpour, another fear knifed through her. Was this the Detroit freeway where people were car-jacked...or worse?

The sky remained slate-gray, and the rain gave no sign of letting up. With a sigh, Jess harnessed her fortitude, then reached down and pulled the trunk-release. Maybe, something in there would look familiar.

While vehicles sailed past sending rooster-tail sprays, Jess stepped into the pelting rain, envisioning her new, colorful umbrella at home on a closet hook.

Drenched within seconds, she lifted the trunk lid and stared inside. An ice scraper gazed back at her.

Rivulets of water ran from her hair and down her face, joining the tears that crept from her eyes. She felt like a weepy child as she looked down at her rain-soaked cotton blouse clinging to her like plastic wrap.

Headlights lit the inside of her trunk. Jess swung around and stared at the halting SUV with panic. Had the driver stopped to offer help...or doom?

A tall, strapping male slid from behind the wheel, deftly unfurling a black umbrella. Silhouetted in the headlights, his broad, athletic shoulders, like a giant, jutted beyond the waterproof shelter.

Anxiously trying to catch a glimpse of his face, she peered at the stranger stepping across the expanding puddles and asked herself a question. Would a thief use an umbrella? Not likely.

"Problem?" he asked, capturing her beneath the waterproof canopy. A fresh, woodsy smell wrapped around her as faced him, nose to broad chest. She cringed as her usually bouncy hair adhered to her wet scalp.

"A flat," she answered, viewing a flash of his chiseled good looks in the passing lights through the blur of rain. She pointed to her back tire. "I don't seem to have a spare or one of those...pump things."

His eyes crinkled, taunting her with a sense of familiarity. "A pump thing?" he asked.

She searched his face and demonstrated with her hand. "You know, one of those gadgets that lifts the car."

"A jack?" His full, resonant voice rippled with good humor.

Humiliated, she glued her attention to the flat, sensing that her mascara had probably made an ugly black trail down her cheeks. "A jack," she mumbled.

But her worry was pointless. The man wasn't looking at her face. Instead, he'd focused on her drenched blouse that clung to her figure with such detail he didn't need an imagination. She gaped at her clearly visible breasts, punctuated by tiny nubs, then raised her hand to cover herself.

When she did, his attention darted upward, and a grin flickered across his face. "Guess I'd better find your 'pump thing.' Will you hold the umbrella?"

Using her free hand, she grasped the handle and held it above him.

Reaching into the trunk, he lifted a section of the floor to reveal, to her surprise, a tire and jack. "Why, look what we have here," he said, eyeing her over his shoulder.

She squirmed, mortified that she had no concept of car repair. "Thanks. Now I know where to look." She'd definitely put car maintenance on her "to do" list. At twenty-eight, the time to learn had come.

"Too bad you picked such a rotten day for a flat. Otherwise, I'd give you a lesson." He turned back to the tire and hoisted it to the trunk edge.

Had he read her mind? Jess's gaze swept across his broad back and down his corded triceps. From him, she might enjoy a lesson.

Astounded at her wayward thoughts, Jess jammed

the pitiful fantasy into her mental wastebasket. She'd been tied to her flourishing catering business for a long time, bound in the kitchen with dough-sticky fingers and a flour-coated body. Dating wasn't on her menu.

When Jess refocused, she faltered at the sodden vision of rain rolling down the stranger's arm and dripping from his elbow. Where would she have been without him? "I'm sorry you've gotten so wet. I can't tell you how grateful I am that you didn't pass me by…like so many others."

He pivoted. "Don't think I didn't consider it, but I'm too much of a gentleman." He gave her a wink while his teasing blue eyes sent her pulse on a sprint.

The man was truly a gentleman, and she chuckled, thinking of her earlier fear. "When you first pulled up, I worried you might be a mugger."

He dropped the tire to the ground, and she followed its descent, then let her gaze wander upward to his trim hips and taut belly beneath his form-fitted jeans.

"Disappointed?" he asked.

She snapped her head upward, then noticed his eyes were on what she'd been inspecting—the area below his waist. A hot flush rose up her neck. "Disappointed? I'm not sure what you mean."

One corner of his mouth lifted in a wry grin. "Disappointed I'm not a mugger?"

"Oh, only a little," she countered, shooting back her movie-starlet smile—a humiliated-starlet smile.

He didn't move, and for a moment a strange sense

of recognition washed over her. She studied him, then mentally shook her head. No. Couldn't be.

Crouching beside the wheel, he hesitated as if waiting for something. "The umbrella keeping you dry?"

"Not really," she said. Then his meaning sank into her soggy, thick skull. Her assignment was to hold the umbrella over *his* head, not hers.

She glanced at the umbrella above her and shifted it while he loosened the lug nuts. When he rose, she smugly raised the canopy higher. He attached the jack, hoisting the car a few inches off the ground.

But soon she lost interest in the tire and umbrella and found herself concentrating on his long, powerful legs bound by drenched, well-worn jeans as tight as adhesive tape. The denim mounted his thighs, nestled around his tight bottom and ended just above his trim hips.

Uncomfortable with her ogling, Jess pulled her attention back to the tire, facing the fact that dating should become part of her agenda.

The man gave the tire a pat and looked up at her. "I wouldn't trust that spare. Looks like dry rot to me." He rose and tossed the muddy tire into the trunk. "I'd get this baby fixed right away."

In a flash, he disengaged the jack and threw it inside, then slammed the lid. "That'll keep for a short time."

His eyes narrowed, scanning her face like a searchlight, and his mouth opened as if wanting to ask her a question, but closed again, curving to a pleasant grin.

"Thanks so much," she said, watching the rain drip from his chin. She'd never had anyone this good-looking…

Jess stopped in midthought. She'd never had anyone be as *chivalrous* as this stranger. Then her manners tugged at her brain. "Let me give you something for your help."

"Okay," he said without hesitation and extended his hand.

Expecting a "no thanks," she reined in her surprised gape. Digging into her shoulder bag for her wallet, Jess heard him laugh. She faltered and looked up.

"I'll settle for my umbrella," he said.

She lifted her gaze above his outstretched hand and peered above her head, staring at the black cloth protecting her from the downpour while he waited like Neptune risen from the sea. She handed the umbrella to him. "Sorry. I seem to have a short attention span."

"Really? I hadn't noticed." He grasped the handle and, with a wave, vanished into his SUV as quickly as he'd appeared. But instead of driving off, he sat with the engine running, apparently waiting for her to leave first.

Chivalry was still alive. Waterlogged, she stepped over a puddle and climbed into her car, realizing she'd let the man of her dreams slip through her fingers before she'd even laid a hand on him. Grinning at the ridiculous fantasy, she pulled into the flow of traffic.

* * *

Derek watched the sedan pull away and gain speed, spewing rainwater in an arched spray from its tires. She was an attractive woman. A beautiful woman— and strangely familiar. Except for her curvy figure beneath the wet clothes, she vaguely resembled his sister's string-bean high-school friend who'd been as shapely as a tube sock.

Not the woman's figure, but her almond-shaped, hazel eyes were etched into his brain. Even more, his memory clung to her full lips, not pouty, but generous and soft. Pliable and temptingly kissable.

He'd opened his mouth to ask her if she happened to be Jess, but he'd stopped himself, fearing his question would sound like the old pickup line "Haven't we met somewhere before?"

Doubting that Jess could ever grow into the shapely mermaid he'd just rescued, he chuckled at his romantic delusion and brushed the thoughts aside, amazed at the yearning that settled deep in his belly.

When Derek thought of romance, his present situation came to mind, and he didn't like what he saw. Gerald Holmes had hired him to work at the television studio, but the man's beautiful daughter had become his nightmare. He'd made a blunder when he'd first come onboard, taking her out a couple of times. He'd backed off, but she hadn't.

Since Holmes had promoted him from gofer to copy editor to an on-the-street reporter over the past few years, he'd begun to wonder if the promotion was success or Patricia's urging.

Derek cringed, admitting his old insecurity sometimes poked at him. In high school he'd knocked 'em dead playing football, but he'd felt awkward and fat, hiding his discomfort with humor and roughhousing. Sports had been his forte—not girls. In college his football talent hadn't been good enough for a pro bid like some of his teammates. Instead he'd found his niche in broadcasting and gained confidence.

Today Derek couldn't deny his success. From viewer fan mail, he'd been called talented, charming and handsome. Apparently on television he appeared self-assured and polished. He'd found success as a TV reporter announcing breaking news to viewers, and he was admired by both men and women.

Maybe that was what had drawn him to the rain-soaked vision he'd stopped to help. He was her hero for only one reason: he was the man who saved her from muggers and carjackers. The man who knew how to change a tire.

Since his early years, he had trimmed down and muscled up, and stood in front of TV cameras with poise and confidence, but inside, when something meant the world to him, Derek often saw himself as the paunchy clown who knew everything about football, but nothing about women.

Jess spotted the You Are Now Entering Royal Oak sign. Following Eleven Mile Road, she made the familiar turns to Maple Street while memories swept over her. She and Meg had spent many girlhood days ambling down this road and sharing their dreams.

Since Jess's parents had moved to Arizona and her brother to Colorado, nothing had coaxed Jess to return...until now.

Pulling in front of the neat, yellow, Cape Cod home, Jess was pleased that the downpour had shifted to a drizzle. When she turned off the ignition and opened the car door, Meg dashed from the house, an umbrella wavering over her head.

"Jess!" Meg called, racing down the walk to meet her.

Bounding from the sedan, Jess ignored her supposed maturity and released a teenager's fan-club scream as she opened her arms to her friend.

Meg rushed into them, the umbrella flailing above her head, and pulled Jess into a hug. Then in a flash, Meg dropped her hold and pranced backward. "Yuck! What happened to you?"

"I had a flat on the freeway." Jess gazed at her trim, fashionable friend, positive she looked like a rag doll in comparison.

"How awful!" Meg said.

"Except for the hunk who stopped to help me." Jess felt as if she was back in the eleventh grade.

Meg's eyes widened. "Really? And...his name?"

Jess shrugged. "When you're drowning, you don't ask."

"Bad news, Jess." Meg opened her palm upward beyond the umbrella, feeling for rain. It had stopped completely, so she lowered and folded the umbrella in one swift movement. "I always had to nudge you along, didn't I?"

Jess nodded. It was true. Meg had a way with men that she envied. Her flowing red hair and green eyes drew men to her like warm cherry pie à la mode.

"But look at you now. You're gorgeous," Meg said, wrapping an arm around her shoulders.

"Thanks," Jess said, ranking her own charm somewhere between pickled beets and boiled okra. "But look at you. Famous New York author. I'm so impressed." She gave Meg an admiring smile and opened the rear door.

"Not famous, but working on it. Now, let's get the luggage in while the rain's let up. I'm sure you'd like to change out of your wetsuit." She pulled out Jess's hanging bag, and Jess grabbed her suitcase and followed her friend's familiar laugh into the house.

"I readied a room upstairs," Meg said, carrying her bag toward the staircase. "While you change, I'll make some hot tea."

"Tea sounds great," Jess said, hauling her suitcase up the steps behind her.

Meg opened the door to the room and sighed. "Derek should really fix this up into a nice guest room."

Jess scanned her surroundings. The room held a few remnants of Derek's past: a college pennant, a bookshelf filled with football trophies and framed photos.

"Derek moved his bedroom downstairs," Meg went on, "and pretty much ignores this part of the house—unless I come to visit."

Meg's bad news skittered into Jess's thoughts. "I'm so sorry about your divorce, Meg. I wish—"

"Don't be sorry." Meg waved her hand as if erasing the thought. "It's water under the Brooklyn Bridge." She gave Jess a brave smile.

Afraid to say any more, Jess squeezed her friend's shoulder and dropped the subject.

Stepping to a scarred dresser, Meg gave it a pat. "I cleared out a couple of drawers, and there's plenty of space in the closet."

"Hey, it beats renting a motel room." But an uneasy feeling rose in her. "Where is Derek, by the way?"

"I'm not sure, but he'll show up eventually." Meg paused in the doorway. "It's good to see you, Jess." She gave the doorjamb a tap. "Okay, I'll go make the tea while you get cleaned up."

"Right," Jess said, wincing as she eyed herself in the mirror. "I look a mess."

Meg sent her a grin, and when she vanished from the doorway, her chuckle echoed down the hallway.

Jess turned back to the mirror. "Mess" wasn't even the word. "Scary" was more like it. Her makeup had vanished except for the dark raccoon rings around her eyes, and her hair hung like a limp mop.

After hanging the clothing bag in the closet, Jess set her suitcase on the bed, opened the lid and pulled out a dry bra and panties. Locating her robe, she pulled it on and turned toward the doorway. She stopped short at the framed photograph on the shelf in front of her.

She dropped the garments on the bed, grabbed the photo and stared at it—a picture of her in a headlock under Derek's meaty teenage arm. Yes. That was how she remembered Derek.

Returning it to the shelf, she picked up another— Derek dressed in his football gear, holding a trophy. Unsettled again, she eyed a smaller photograph tucked into the edge of the frame—her senior picture. She swallowed her surprise. Why had Derek displayed her photo?

Filled with questions, Jess hopped into the shower. When she'd finished and dried, she slipped on her teal spandex pants and an oversize matching-print T-shirt. Running a comb through her damp hair, she took a final puzzled peek at the photographs and headed downstairs.

Meg greeted her in the living room with the promised tea and a plate of Oreos. They curled up in chairs, gabbing and giggling just as they'd done in the past— until the tangy scent of cooking food drifted from the kitchen. Jess sniffed the air.

Meg glanced at her wristwatch. "Let me check the casserole, then I'll bring back the teapot for a refill." Heading toward the door, she called over her shoulder, "Dinner's nothing fancy."

Fancy or not, Jess didn't care. She was hungry and the aroma had aroused her taste buds. With Meg in the kitchen, Jess relaxed against the chair and took in the room. The familiar setting sparked memories:

gabfests, sleepovers, cramming for exams... She warmed, remembering them all.

The sound of a door slamming jarred her thoughts. A man's voice rumbled from the kitchen, and she unconsciously pushed herself deep into the cushions of the chair, hoping to be invisible if the intruder was Derek...and she was pretty certain it was.

Meg's voice piped up from the distance. "I knew you'd get home when you smelled food."

"Just your good cooking," he said.

Jess liked the sound of Derek's deep, resonant voice. Her curiosity won out, and she leaned toward the doorway, hoping to get a glimpse of the adult hulk.

Something metal, like a pot lid, clanked, then Meg gasped. "What happened to you? You look like a car wreck."

Derek chuckled before his response sailed into the living room. "Believe it or not, I was out playing 'knight in shining armor' on the freeway."

On the freeway. The memory of gorgeous eyes filled Jess's thoughts, and she stopped breathing. *No. Impossible.*

She heard the refrigerator door close. "Whose car's in front? It looks familiar," he asked, sounding as if his mouth was full of food.

"It's Jess's. And stop eating, Derek. It's time for dinner as soon as I make a salad." Her voice was hushed, but Jess heard, anyway. "I told you she was coming for the centennial. She's in the living room."

Jess grinned. Did Meg think she was deaf?

"Hey, Frenchie!" Derek boomed.

"Don't start that, Derek," Meg said in another stage whisper. "Try 'Jess.' You'll get along much better."

Derek's new greeting, "Hey, String Bean," sailed into the room only a pulse beat before his body.

Jess took a deep breath and looked toward the door, wondering if it could really be. When she saw those eyes and that build, her heart skipped. He skidded to a halt.

Chapter Two

"It *was* you!" Derek and Jess said in unison.

His sudden stop sent a slosh of milk and an Oreo cookie to the floor, but he didn't move. He couldn't take his eyes off the vision he'd met on the freeway.

The cookie rolled across the carpet and stopped at her feet while his gaze journeyed upward along a stretch of slender leg to a shapely body hidden beneath an oversize T-shirt. When he reached her face, it looked as amazed as he felt.

As he scrambled for composure, his memory conjured up the image of his sister's skinny, giggling high-school girlfriend, a beanpole with straight, dark hair and huge lovely eyes.

She was still graced with those beautiful eyes, canopied by dark, long lashes and a gently curved brow. Her beanpole figure had aged better than fine burgundy. Though right now her shape was hidden, he recalled the curvaceous figure in the wet blouse he'd enjoyed earlier that day.

He closed his gaping mouth and swallowed. "What happened to you, Jess? I thought you looked familiar earlier, but I couldn't imagine it was really you."

He said goodbye to the taunting String Bean nickname, and the name Frenchie wavered in his throat. Considering her French surname and those full lips, which triggered a sensation in his gut, the nickname still held promise.

Realizing she hadn't responded, he shifted his appraising eyes. "You didn't forget me, did you?"

"How could I?"

Though she rolled her eyes before sending him a wry grin, the muscles in his belly tightened, adding to the other lingering sensation.

"It's like asking me if I forgot the black plague," she said.

His motor skills returning, he propelled his legs to her side and bent down to snatch up the escaped Oreo. He slipped his arm around her shoulders, to give her a friendly squeeze, but the contact sent his heart leaping like a yo-yo. "I wasn't that bad, was I?"

"Don't ask." Her voice resounded with playful sarcasm.

He had been and he knew it. "We were kids then," Derek said. "I'm twenty-six. Not sixteen."

"I'm twenty-eight," Jess said, her voice fading. "My birthday was last month."

"Happy birthday," Derek said. "You don't look a day over twenty-five."

Jess gave a grudging thank-you.

"Since that's settled, let's shake and forget the past. Think about the gallant gentleman who changed your tire and didn't drive off with your car."

Derek withdrew his arm from around her shoulders, not wanting to push his luck, and extended his hand. Spotting cookie residue, he wiped his fingers on his mud-speckled jeans and reached toward her again.

She accepted the gesture. "I'll shake, Derek, but I'm not promising anything. You'll have to prove yourself."

Lingering with her warm hand in his, Derek grinned. "I'll enjoy that, Jess."

She appeared to think that over for a heartbeat, then pulled away as a pink flush tinted her cheeks. "You were very nice to me this afternoon when I was a stranger, but now, I'm just old Frenchie. I'll believe it when I see it. Or rather, hear it."

He let his gaze linger on her lips for a moment before pushing his thoughts aside. He'd been a jerk years ago. He definitely needed to create a new image. "Not *old* Frenchie, Jess," he said. "You look brand-new to me. You look great. It's really good to see you."

She frowned as if weighing his words until her scowl turned to an amiable smile. "Thanks. I assume that was a compliment."

"From the heart," he said, surprised to realize he meant every word. Pleasure coursed through him as he anticipated her company for the rest of the evening. But then he remembered. In his enthusiasm, he'd forgotten he had a staff meeting tonight. Sitting at the studio was no way to spend his time when a lovely woman graced his living room.

Feeling his stomach rumble, Derek took a step backward. "Before I say more than I should, I'm going to check on dinner." He delivered his best TV-personality wink. "But we'll talk later." The line, one he'd used on female fans at public appearances, rang as tinny as a cowbell. He was sure Jess recognized it as such when she gave him the sort of look that women give worms washed onto the sidewalk after a hard spring rain.

Sucking in a deep breath, Derek left the room, grateful for time to think. He needed a game plan if he had any hope of getting Jess to trust him now that she'd reappeared in his life.

He paused at the kitchen door. Why did he care what she thought? Ten years had passed since they'd last seen each other. Ten years that had changed them both. And from what he'd learned from Meg, Jess had made her dream come true. She had become a self-assured, successful businesswoman, while he was still struggling to reach his goal at the station.

Hit by reality, he dropped the ball at the fifty-yard line. *Who are you fooling, Derek?* The old shaky confidence jangled his nerves. Maybe, instead, he'd forget a game plan and just punt.

Jess stood in the living room alone, her stomach full and her mind confused. Meg's chicken casserole had been excellent, and their talk had been of old

friends and funny school memories. While Derek
changed clothes and Meg cleaned the kitchen refusing
help—as usual—Jess was left with her thoughts.

Jess had watched Derek at dinner, remembering
how she'd been niggled with a strange sense of familiarity earlier that day, and she recalled with ad-
miration his corded arms and firm legs as he changed
her tire. He'd seemed witty and charming. Her highway hero.

Derek? A hero? She shook her head. Her emotions
tumbled through her like clothes in a dryer.

Alone now, she wandered across the room, hoping
to dislodge her discomfort. She paused to look at the
display of family photos, thumbed through a stack of
books on a shelf and gazed nostalgically at the view
from the large picture window before moving to the
sofa and sinking onto it.

Intent on her thoughts, she flinched when she
looked up to see Derek, his clothes changed, observ-
ing her from the doorway. He ambled into the room
and sat on the cushion beside her.

"So...now that we have the preliminary greetings
out of the way, let's talk about us," he said.

"Us?" Jess was taken aback. "Why not tell me
about you? Why are you still in Royal Oak? I thought
you'd be butting heads with the Packers or Rams,"
she said, picturing the old Derek charging down the
field, thick legs pumping, the football tucked against
his paunchy belly.

Her question seemed to disconcert him, and Jess
was sorry she asked.

"I did play ball at Michigan State...but I became involved in broadcasting."

"Broadcasting?" His rich, distinctive voice filled her ears, and she could almost hear him as a late-evening deejay.

"I'm a TV newsman. Channel 5. Surprised?"

TV newsman? Jess reeled with the idea. "A little," she said, lying through her teeth. Since he'd bounded into the living room with his milk and cookies, Jess had spent her time trying to change her image of him as a six-foot-two beefy teenager to the lean, handsome, thoughtful man who'd changed her tire.

"So that's why you're still here in your folks' house," Jess said with a sweep of her arm. Her words struck her and she corrected herself. "I mean...your house. Meg said you bought it."

Derek nodded. "I bought Meg's share. Mom left it to us when she died. I suppose I'm still here because it's home."

Because it's home. Jess's mind filled with memories. "After Meg called a few weeks ago, I began thinking about your folks. I remember your dad died and now..." She faltered, recalling his good-natured, supportive parents and feeling the pull of emotion. "I'm really sorry about your mom, Derek."

"Thanks," he said.

Silence hung on the air and Jess struggled to direct her thoughts, wanting to get back to something less depressing.

"You came home for the centennial," Derek said, jarring the quiet. "I'm glad. It should be fun."

You came home. His words hit a chord. No matter how long Jess had lived in Cincinnati, the city was never home. Her heart had snagged on the little town of Royal Oak and stayed there. Her life had been full and her ego delicate back then.

"I miss this town." She lifted her eyes to his, and time stood still. Derek, the pest from her past, was sending her emotions on an uneven spin.

Overtired—that was it. She'd driven nearly three hundred miles, feared a mugging on the freeway, met a Prince Charming...who turned out to be the man playing hopscotch with her heart.

"Why not move back?" he asked.

Before she could conjure up an answer, Meg stepped into the room, carrying a carafe of coffee. She set a mug in front of Jess and handed another to Derek.

Derek took a sip, then leaned back and asked his question again. "Why not move back?"

"Because I have a business in Cincinnati."

"She does catering," Meg said.

Jess nodded. "Fresh Beginnings."

"Fresh Beginnings? Fascinating name," Derek said. "Tell me about it."

Wondering if he was taunting her, she feared looking too deeply into his eyes. Yet only interest filled his face. Flustered, she hesitated. How long would it take her to trust Derek? "My partner and I thought it was a good name since our speciality is hors d'oeuvres."

He tilted his head as if in question.

"Appetizers. Canapés," she explained, not sure he understood. "You eat them before a meal…or sometimes at a party."

His face brightened with amusement, and she felt duped by his silence. "You know what I mean," she said in frustration.

He chuckled. "You mean people actually eat those little things?"

She peered at him, deciding whether to respond or ignore his teasing. She went for ignore and changed the subject. "So tell me about the centennial celebration."

"They've planned a lot of events," Derek said. "Channel 5's doing a big spread on it all. Since I'm from Royal Oak—" he cleared his throat "—and no one else wanted the assignment, I volunteered to do some special spots. You know, impress the boss."

Time for her to do the taunting. Jess tossed back a wry "You mean you have to work at impressing people?"

He chucked her under the chin. "I won't answer that."

Her skin warmed at his touch and she grappled with the unexpected sensation. "I didn't mean to distract you," she said, knowing that she was the one distracted. "Let's get back to the centennial. Besides the television spread, what's happening?"

He grinned. "Let's see. They're having…"

He looked toward Meg as if for help, but she took a slow sip of coffee and remained decidedly quiet.

"…a parade," he continued without her help, "and

a tour of the new high-school facilities. Oh, and a football game.'' He turned to his sister again. ''What else, Meg?''

''A reception,'' she replied.

''Sounds like fun,'' Jess said.

''And a dance to end the celebration.'' He lifted his mug and took a sip, his eyes riveted to Jess's.

''Dance,'' she parroted. Her emotions took flight again, like startled birds.

As he had in the past, Derek seemed to fluster her, but instead of frustration, he was rousing warm feelings in the pit of her stomach—feelings she'd overlooked for too long.

''Do you like to dance?'' Derek's soft, husky voice washed over her.

Dance? How long had it been? ''Sure, but it's been years. I've probably forgotten how.'' She'd also forgotten to bring clothes dressy enough for a dance.

''I'd be happy to give you a refresher co—''

''Derek,'' Meg interrupted, ''I thought you had a meeting tonight.''

He gave his sister a quick scowl, then covered it with a crooked grin. ''I'd rather be here,'' he said close to Jess's ear.

Looking into Derek's eyes, Jess felt her heart somersault. They were the brilliant blue of a Caribbean lagoon, and she couldn't pull her gaze away. Watching the amused look creep over Derek's face, she figured he knew she couldn't look away. Distrust rifled through her. She recognized his old maneuver.

''Hello,'' Meg sang.

Jess turned toward her friend and saw her eyeing them with curiosity tattooed on her face.

"Am I interrupting?" Meg asked.

"Not at all," Jess said, thinking it was a good thing she had.

Derek cleared his throat. "I think she did." He leaned nearer and slid his arm around Jess's shoulders. "You bring out the worst in me, Jess," he said under his breath. "You always did. I acted like a fool when we were teenagers and—"

The telephone's ring stopped his confession in midsentence and didn't allow her to tell him he hadn't changed one iota. But she knew he had.

"You get it, Derek," Meg said. "I'm sure it's for you."

Derek kept his eyes focused on Jess, his arm cuddled around her shoulder. "It's your turn, Meg."

"My turn?" Meg flashed him a quizzical look. Instead of waiting for a response, she grabbed the carafe and hurried into the kitchen.

Derek shifted closer. "We haven't talked in so long, Jess. I'd really like to hear more about you…and your business. It sounds—"

"Derek," Meg called from the kitchen, "it's for you. Patricia."

"Patricia?" Derek looked distinctly uncomfortable. "I'll be right back." He took his hand from Jess's arm and headed for the kitchen.

Uncertainty niggled at Jess. At present her love life was basically nil. Sure, she looked at men, occasionally had vague dreams, but this new Derek stirred up a vivid sense of awareness she hadn't counted on. He'd become a tall, strapping specimen of handsome masculinity. And Jessamy Cosette had never allowed herself, in the interest of science, to close her eyes to an intriguing specimen. And an appealing one at that.

Yet somewhere between appeal and curiosity, old recollections haunted her: his unmerciful heckling, hovering and teasing. Could she trust him now? Was he toying with her emotions the way he did years ago? Still, on the freeway he'd been not only captivating but sincerely kind.

The discrepancy jabbed at her senses. Seeing was not believing, after all. She wondered where the real Derek began and ended. Compared to Jess and her skepticism, "Doubting Thomas" was an amateur.

Meg returned to the living room with fresh coffee and pulled Jess from her thoughts. "I see Derek is weaving his spell over you. I can't believe it." She refreshed their cups, then set the carafe on the table.

"What do you mean? He's just being nice, Meg. And so am I. I can't let the past linger forever. He was a jerk then, but he isn't now."

Meg plopped into the chair and leaned against the cushion. She took a long, slow sip of coffee before speaking. "I always thought Derek had a thing for you."

"Me?" Jess blinked, then let out a hoot. "You're kidding!"

"Hey, I'm his older sister. How could he admit he lusted after my best friend? Anyway, he was an oaf back then."

Meg tucked her shoulders upward toward her ears and pitched her voice low. "On the field. Number Thirty-three. Big Derek, the derrick!" Her titters ended the impersonation. "I remember his buddies pushing him to date Patti Pompom while he clung to every word I said about you."

"He was just a kid," Jess said. But remembering the bedroom photos, a prickle of speculation tingled up her arms. "I couldn't stand him, remember?" Uneasy, Jess concentrated on her coffee mug.

Meg grinned. "How could I forget?"

"Forget what?" Derek asked, striding back into the room. He sat in his vacated spot on the sofa beside Jess. "So, where did we leave off?"

Jess choked on her swallow of wine. "About ten years ago, I think." She chuckled.

Meg joined her.

"I don't get it, you two," he said, looking from one to the other.

Meg shook her head. "Come on, Derek. You remember how you behaved around Jess, don't you?"

Watching Derek's confused, then embarrassed reaction as his sister reminded him, Jess almost felt sorry for him.

"You two must have overdosed on caffeine," Derek said. He gulped down the rest of his coffee, then set the mug on the table and rose. "I have to leave you ladies to fend for yourselves."

Meg rolled her eyes. "Heaven forbid."

Ignoring his sister, Derek put his hands on Jess's shoulders and bent close to her ear. "I'm sorry Jess—

I'd like to visit.'' He pulled back and looked directly into her eyes. "I mean that.''

Addled by her reaction, Jess said nothing. But she did want to learn more about the new-and-improved Derek.

She stared at the doorway for a long moment after he left, as mottled emotions settled over her. She imagined someone named Patricia waiting somewhere, anxious to run her fingers through Derek's thick, waving bronze hair, as well as do a few other things Jess didn't even want to think about. She hated the alien feeling of jealousy that ransacked her.

Meg cleared her throat, and Jess pulled her gaze from the doorway.

"Are they an item? Derek and Patricia?" Jess asked, praying Meg wouldn't say yes.

Chapter Three

Derek crept into the darkened house and snapped on the kitchen light. The evening had been more than stressful. While the station worked toward syndicating one of their programs, the staff had been under Patricia's manicured thumb, planning short- and long-range promotional strategies.

For some time he'd had his fill of the way Patricia controlled the station, and if he had any guts, he'd either deal with her father or walk away gracefully. Tonight when the meeting ended, Patricia had nabbed him. She'd contrived the need for a ride home and suggested they go out for a drink before dropping by her place.

He had given her the ride, gone for the drink, but received a tongue-lashing when he'd dropped her off and hurried away, longing to get home to his house-guest. Though Jess challenged him, he sensed something else about her as they talked. Awareness. Confusion.

He cringed. He'd been a jerk—taunting Jess with cruel nicknames, grabbing her in headlocks, hanging around like a pesky puppy. In truth, he'd been crazy about her. He'd found her fascinating. And now she was gorgeous, as well.

Earlier while they had eaten Meg's casserole, he'd only nibbled, distracted by Jess's intoxicating eyes. Now his stomach growled, demanding food. Opening the refrigerator door, Derek leaned inside, gazing at his options. Meg had been thoughtful and filled it in anticipation of Jess's visit, so his gaze feasted on sliced roast beef and ham from the deli, a thick block of jack cheese, a dozen eggs, a slab of bacon.

He glanced at his watch—2:00 a.m. Breakfast seemed fitting. He grabbed two eggs, but when he swung around, his heart lurched and an egg tumbled from his hand to go *splat* on the floor.

Curious hazel eyes watched him from the doorway. "Thought you were a prowler," Jess said. "But I was wrong. Only a six-foot-plus klutz." Her focus shifted to the floor.

"Good morning." He grabbed a section of paper towel with his free hand and wiped up the egg.

She eyed her empty wrist, then searched the kitchen until she found the wall clock. "I suppose you could call it morning. I'd say middle of the night myself." She wandered into the room and sat on a kitchen chair, propping one slippered foot over the other. "Hungry?"

"Famished. Ravenous." His gaze lingered on her tempting form.

"Your lady friend didn't feed you?"

Her comment jerked him to attention. "Trust me, Patricia is not my lady friend. She's the boss's daughter. I tend to tread lightly, but lately my steel-toed boots want to do some stomping."

"Sounds scary. Are you the big bad wolf?"

"I'm not telling. I'd ruin my lamb disguise. But let's not talk about Patricia."

Facing her, he stood transfixed, studying her clean, unadorned face looking soft and sleepy-eyed. His pulse slipped into second gear, and his emotions, though dead only an hour earlier, stirred soft and warm in his belly like a litter of kittens.

"Care to join me? Scrambled eggs with ham and cheese. How does that sound?" he asked, directing the conversation to safer ground.

"Are you using a bowl?" She looked pointedly at the moist spot still obvious on the floor.

"That's not a bad idea."

She laughed and unfolded herself from the chair. "How about if I help?"

They worked side by side whipping eggs, chopping ham and grating cheese. A warm, amiable feeling wrapped around him like a love song.

Jess poured orange juice, and he found some instant coffee, rather than making a full pot and arousing Meg with the drifting aroma. Finally they sat across from each other at the kitchen table and plowed into the early-morning breakfast.

His gaze slid over her as she forked the egg into her mouth. She lifted the paper napkin and dabbed her naturally rosy lips, so soft and full he had to look away for a moment. She hadn't needed the napkin, but the action seemed as natural as her glowing skin.

He felt stupid, mesmerized by her use of a napkin. It had taken him a while to finally grow up enough to use one himself.

"It's been ten years," he said, yanking himself from the humiliating picture of his youthful primitive table manners. "That's a long time. People change. Look at you."

"And look at you." She glanced down shyly at her robe and slippers. "Who'd have thought I'd be sitting here in your folks' old house in my robe, eating breakfast again after all these years?"

"And with me," he added, figuring she was saying that in her head.

She grinned as if he'd hit the mark. "And with you," she repeated.

He wiped his mouth with the napkin, hoping she noticed. "Tell me about you. I'm curious about how you got started in the catering business."

"Not much to tell. College, changing majors, graduation, realizing I picked the wrong career, back to college. Not too exciting."

"Marriage?"

"Almost, but no." She paused, searching his face. "You?"

"No. Never found the right woman."

She chuckled, then locked her eyes to his. "Or, as I suspect, found too many women."

"No," he said, shaking his head—hopefully not so quickly that he looked guilty. "Too busy in college. Not that I didn't date, but nothing serious."

Looking at Jess, he concluded that he may have found the right woman years ago. "Then after I graduated," he continued, "I spent time working my way up in broadcasting. Two years in radio, now television. The job eats your hours."

She nodded as if she understood.

"Morning, afternoon, night," he continued. "Grab some sleep, then back to the studio. Midnight shift. Mornings. And I mean mornings, like 3:00 a.m. to get ready for a 6:00 a.m. newscast and..." Hearing himself ramble, he halted. "I asked about you, and here I am talking about me. So tell me about the 'almost.'"

"The what?" She wrinkled her brow and tilted her head, her dark-brown hair splaying over her shoulder.

"The 'almost got married.'" He leaned back in the chair, cradling his coffee mug in his hands and admiring her sweet, titillating appearance in bathrobe and slippers.

"Oh, *that* 'almost.'" She smiled. "I graduated in business and met him the first place I worked. You know, Mr. Executive. Polished, urbane, important. I finally realized he wasn't meant for me."

"You didn't like the 'polished' part?"

"Polished, I like. His tedium bothered me the most," she said, "and his self-promotion."

He decided to leave well enough alone and not make contrasts. "How did you end up in catering?"

"I didn't enjoy the marketing job I had. So I did a career search. I had the business degree and decided I'd like to be my own boss. I stumbled into catering. I always loved to cook. I'd taken some elective cooking classes at the college—just for fun. I added a few courses and voilà. Catering." Her eyes sparkled as she spoke.

"So you didn't start your business right out of college?"

"No, after the marketing firm, I worked for a catering company for a few months for the experience, then a woman I met in college wanted to start up a business. She didn't have a lot of time, but had the money. I didn't have money, but I had the time. So here I am."

"Why just those little pop-one-in-the-mouth guys? Where's the gourmet steak?"

A tiny grin tugged at her mouth. "There's a big business in hors d'oeuvres. Most corporations and company parties prefer them, and wealthy executives giving cocktail parties want finger foods. Not as much overhead for me." She took a breath. "I'd like to expand one day...but my partner isn't too eager."

"Why not?" Derek asked.

"She doesn't like the extra work. She put up the money when we first began and I did the work—but now, financially I'm a full partner. She still likes the original arrangement. She provides the money, I do the work." She shrugged. "Oh well, with the canapés lots can be partially prepared the day before. And I can do many things the same evening as the party.''

"In the evening? You're too pretty to be spending your evenings making horse doovers.'' He waited, hoping she'd give him a full smile. She did. His pulse went into overdrive.

"Thanks. But I don't think 'pretty' is quite the word.'' She opened her arms, pivoting from the waist back and forth, giving him a visual.

Despite her humor, the picture was wonderful. Her dark hair framed the fairest skin he'd ever seen, sweetened by a natural pink flush in her cheeks and lips. "Okay, pretty isn't the word,'' he said. "How about beautiful?''

She leaned across the table and scowled. "You're overtired. You're not focusing. And neither am I.''

She rose and carried her plate to the sink, swishing it under the hot water. "I hope we can wash these dishes in the morning.''

Derek cleared his place and stepping up beside her, it was all he could do not to take her in his arms. She seemed so delicate beside him. So fragile. He grinned, thinking that not her size, but her spirit could easily bowl him over. "I'll throw them in the dishwasher. You go ahead.''

He took a chance and caressed her shoulder, fighting his eager inclination to do more. She didn't flinch, but gave him a pleasant look.

"See you in the morning,'' she said. Glancing at the clock, she added, "*Later* in the morning.''

She breezed through the doorway while he leaned

against the sink and caught his breath. He'd have to tie himself to the bedpost or hide out to keep his hands off her. No way could he spend time around Jess and not kiss those luscious lips.

He rubbed his temples, amazed that the girl of his dreams was back in his life…a woman. But how long would she be here? His question pinned him to the spot. Only two weeks.

Jess's life was in Cincinnati and his, in Royal Oak.

When Jess awoke, it took her a moment to remember where she was. Her attention fastened on the line of trophies stretched across the bookcase and she grinned, thinking of the early-morning refrigerator raid.

She and Derek had actually held a conversation. Talked! Her heart skipped at the recollection. The event seemed astounding. Ludicrous. Derek had been a sliver in her finger forever. Now just because he'd become a handsome hunk of flesh—and a seemingly nice hunk at that—she refused to let her imagination run wild.

Jess had her career, and she'd reached her goal, her own business, no one to please but herself and her partner. She'd promised to let nothing get in her way—especially a man. Yet Derek's face lingered in her mind as she dressed and headed for the kitchen.

Meg looked up as Jess came through the doorway. "My, my. Slept a wee bit late this morning, didn't we?" Her facetious comment was altered by the grin on her lips. "I see that you and Mr. Television had a midnight snack."

Jess poured a cup of coffee, covering the heat that sneaked up her neck. "Who are you? Agatha Christie?" Hoping her pink tinge stayed beneath her sweater, she faced Meg. "I thought he was a prowler."

"Sure." Meg leaned against the kitchen counter. "So what did the two of you talk about?"

Jess sat on the same chair she'd sat in a few hours earlier and lifted her eyes to Meg at the counter. "Nothing much. Mostly what we'd been doing for the past ten years."

"Aha, catching up."

Jess sipped her coffee without comment.

"And?"

"And nothing. Don't try to do your romance-nudging on me now. I'm too old. That was in our teen years. I don't need help with romance, dear friend. Your brother has been a pain in my tush for years, and I don't plan to take the pain home with me."

Meg slid into Derek's chair across from her. "Don't get yourself riled. I'm just thinking you'd make a great sister-in-law."

Meg's words untethered the pink she'd kept hidden. The heat rose up her neck to her cheeks despite her deep breath to lasso it back. "Please keep that thought to yourself."

Meg didn't respond, but her Cheshire-cat grin said

more than words. "I'd laugh my rear off, Jess. You and Derek! Unbelievable."

Jess kept her thoughts to herself. No sense in egging her on. Anyway, Meg was correct. It *was* unbelievable.

Meg remained silent for a moment, then changed the subject. "So, what should we do today? I can work at the computer awhile. Or we can chase down old friends. What's your pleasure?"

"I don't want to keep you from your writing. I can entertain myself while you do what you have to do."

"You're not holding me up, Jess. I'm not working on a deadline right now, and I'm thrilled you're here."

"I'd like to make a couple of telephone calls and get organized."

Meg nodded. "That's fine...and at noon, if you'd like, you can catch Derek on the news."

Hearing his name, Jess's heart jumped rope a few skips. Jess swallowed to stop the ridiculous feeling from rising colorfully on her skin. She'd always hated her fair complexion. Every hint of discomfort rose on her face like a flag. "Sure. Can't say I'm not curious."

Meg went about her work, and Jess lingered over the coffee, gazing at the empty chair and reliving the middle of the night tête-à-tête. Finished, she rinsed her cup and climbed the stairs to retrieve her small address book. While in town, she wanted to call a few old friends and make plans. But when her watch hands neared twelve, she lost interest in her project.

Sauntering casually into the living room, Jess snapped on the TV, keeping the volume low. Her efforts were in vain.

"Channel 5," Meg called from the den.

Jess, with as much nonchalance as she could muster, punched the remote. The station break ended and the news theme music blatted from the set. A long desk came into view and the camera panned in. The news anchor related news for a moment, then flashed to a special story.

Gooseflesh prickled down Jess's arms as she gazed at Derek, smiling into the camera and looking far more handsome than she wanted to admit. "This is Derek Randolph on top of the Renaissance Center…"

Jess didn't hear the rest of his message, but only watched and listened to his voice, spellbound. His bronze hair lightened under the beam of lights, and as the camera moved in for a close-up, his eyes sparkled for the viewers. Jess imagined he had a whole fan club of women dashing for the TV to see his gorgeous smiling eyes.

Near the end of the broadcast, Meg wandered into the living room carrying a sheet of paper and sat on the arm of the sofa. The theme music ended the show, and Meg cleared her throat. "Didn't want to disturb you while you were captivated by Mr. Charming." She tittered.

"Would you stop that!" Jess gave her an evil eye, but had to admit she was absolutely right. Derek had mesmerized her.

Meg dropped the paper into Jess's lap. "E-mail,"

she said. "I just checked on-line. A little note to you from you know who."

Jess gazed down and saw Derek's name. Her focus jumped up to the brief message: *How about lunch, and I can show you the studio. Have Sis e-mail me back.* Jess glanced at her watch. Twelve-thirty. "You want to go, Meg?" She gestured to the note.

"Go where?" Her friend looked at her with blank eyes.

"Come on. Don't tell me you didn't read this thing." She waved the sheet of paper in front of Meg. "To lunch and tour the studio with Derek."

"You think I'd read your private e-mail?"

This time the Cheshire-cat grin belonged to Jess. "Yes."

Meg smiled back and shook her head. "I've been there. Besides, he didn't invite me. The pleasure is all yours."

The pleasure is all yours. Pleasure? Jess wasn't sure. Common sense told her that the bewildering emotions coursing through her would only lead to frustration and disappointment.

Chapter Four

As soon as she arrived at the station, Derek hurried her off to lunch. Inside the restaurant, she admired his handsome features, wondering why she hadn't suspected years ago that despite his teenage quirks, he'd been television material. She recalled him playing deejay while she and Meg tried to listen to the local radio stations. Derek had driven her crazy. Now he was driving her crazy again, but in a much different way.

Enjoying her deli sandwich and avoiding references to the past, Jess kept the conversation casual while her thoughts were riffled with unanswered questions.

Derek spent most of the meal telling her about what she'd see at the studio. "Some bigwigs are coming into town from our New York affiliate. I've been tied up with that project for weeks. We're all feeling a lot of stress until it's finalized. You'll see what I mean once you're at the studio."

"It sounds fascinating," Jess said, but a perplexing question settled in her thoughts.

"Did I tell you about the story I did yesterday?"

Watching his face fill with excitement, she shook her head.

"This is why I love my work." The enthusiasm grew to compassion. "I interviewed a mother whose kidnapped child was recovered—alive and well."

"That's so awesome," Jess said, watching his eyes mist.

"I was touched by the story." He released an embarrassed chuckle. "I had to struggle more than once to keep my emotions under control."

"I don't know how you do it," she said, understanding why he loved his work. "I know the stories aren't always happy ones."

He nodded. "Wish I could say they were."

When they finished, Derek paid the bill, and once outside in the autumn sunshine, Jess inhaled the fresh, rejuvenating air and tossed out the question that had puzzled her. "I don't understand something, Derek. Something you were talking about earlier. Why you?"

His head swiveled and a bewildered look settled on his face. "Why me?"

"Why are you involved in this New York project? You're an on-the-street reporter. Seems as if they'd get one of the top guns." She cringed as the words left her mouth. ''Not to mean you're not tops at what you do.''

Her attempted recovery made Derek grin. ''Thanks. I love backhanded compliments.''

She tugged on the sleeve of his sun-warmed suit coat. ''You know what I mean.''

''I suspect I'm being groomed.''

''Groomed?''

''For a promotion. We've heard rumors for a while that a position is opening for a new anchor. I'm not sure yet which one, but an anchor job is what I dream about.''

''That would be wonderful.'' Her own newly formed idea seeped into her thoughts. Coming home. Selling the business to her partner. It all made sense. ''I'm happy for you.''

''Don't jump the gun. I'm not that confident.''

His voice faded, and the tone prompted another question. ''Why not, Derek? You spend so much time at the station doing all the extra projects and—''

''It's not my time or ability. I give them good stories and meet deadlines. I work hard. It's my competition. A couple of them are one step ahead of me.''

''Ahead of you?''

''They're married.''

His comment brought her to a skidding halt. ''Married? What does that have to do with anything?''

''My boss is a family man. His wife died a few years ago and he dotes on his daughter. He's very candid about his feelings. In his opinion, married men are stable. Married men are dependable. Married men deserve financial rewards.''

''But...that's not necessarily true.'' Jess's head spun with the archaic attitude. ''The man should see that you're all those things.'' Patricia landed in her thoughts like the enemy parachuting onto foreign soil. ''Is it because of his daughter? She's chasing you, and you're not interested. Is that it?''

''I don't think so. Holmes knows his daughter. I think it's just what I said. He doesn't see me settled and established. No wife and kids to keep my nose to the computer. I'm in competition with two other reporters who are married. At least, that's what I figure.''

''Then you should do something about it.'' Though she uttered the words, the thought traveled through her like a virus, gnawing at her stomach.

''Do something?'' He poked his hand into his trouser pocket and fidgeted with his keys. ''Like stop someone on the street and ask her to marry me?''

His perplexed expression roused her spirit. ''Not a stranger, but you must have someone you see occasionally. Maybe someone from the studio, or one of your devoted fans. You could date and look like you're settling down.''

He held her arm loosely. ''How about you? What do you think about marrying me?''

Startled, Jess stumbled over a chunk of raised pavement. Derek made a gallant save and pulled her closer to his side.

"I didn't say marry," Jess countered. "I said date—and I didn't mean me."

"Why not?" He nuzzled against her side. "You're the best woman in town."

"In town for only three weeks." Her words silenced them both until they'd arrived back at the studio. When Derek held open the door, Jess relaxed and a grin settled on her face. During high school he'd held doors *closed*—with both hands—when she tried to enter the building. Would she ever get accustomed to Derek's surprising charm?

"This is my kingdom," he said with a sweep of his arm. He guided her down the hallway, introducing her to co-workers on the way. "Here's where the news staff works—AP bulletins, news briefs, local news—like I explained."

She scanned the large room, full of desks crowded with telephones, monitors, faxes and copy machines, clacking and blinking.

"Computers, instead of the old ticker tapes we used to see on those late-night movies," Derek said with a hint of nostalgia. "Sophisticated stuff now."

Inwardly Jess smiled at his reference to the ancient television movie nights at Meg's.

He steered her across the room to the pleasant-faced gentleman she'd seen earlier on the afternoon news.

"Jess, this is Brian Lowery. Brian, Jess Cosette, a longtime friend."

Brian extended his hand. "Nice to meet you, Jess. Visiting?" He gave her the once-over.

She nodded. "For the centennial. I live in Cincinnati now."

"Too bad," he said with a wink. "For Derek, I mean." He sent her a sly smile.

Covering her discomfort, she laughed. "Derek? Are you kidding? He's my best friend's kid brother."

She gave Derek's forearm a playful pat, and when she lowered her hand, the hard strength of his arm lingered against her fingers.

Derek didn't acknowledge his co-worker's comment and drew Jess's attention to the activity around her. She watched with interest while printers and faxes zipped off sheets of information, reporters worked head to head, and monitors rolled interviews and breaking news.

"Lots going on." She turned to face him. "Did I mention I watched your noon newscast? You did good." His amused eyes sent her pulse skipping.

"You told me at lunch," he said as his expression changed to the knowing grin she was learning to hate.

Jess cleared her throat to hide her chagrin. A groupie. She'd never been one and now wasn't the time to start. "This place is too noisy. I'm getting a headache."

"Follow me," he said, catching her elbow and guiding her down the hall. "I'll show you the place I call my own."

Derek opened a door and motioned Jess inside. "Here's where I hang my hat. But the breaking news is out there. I work on special reports and feature stories in here. It's a little quieter."

Though the noise was muted, the bustle reverberated through a glass window. Jess massaged her temples, wondering if it was the chaos or her unexpected reaction to Derek that had given her the headache.

Looking for something to rid her of fluctuating feelings, she scanned Derek's desk. Anything would help. Photographs of old girlfriends, personal items that might conjure up the old images. A football trophy or two. But she saw nothing except the usual pencil holder, dirty coffee mug, in-out box and computer.

"Sit." He rolled out the chair. "See if you missed your calling."

She sank onto the chair and eyed him.

He peered at her through his thumb and index finger circled to form a make-believe lens. "You'd look great in front of a camera. Has anyone told you that before?"

"No," she said, grasping her old image of him to control her emotions. "And don't try using flattery to wheedle your way onto my 'forgive and forget' list."

His smile sent warmth slithering up her spine, and she struggled without success to hold her own smile at bay.

He leaned forward, bracing his elbows on the desktop, his chin in his hand. He was so close she could smell the mint he'd popped in his mouth as they left the deli. "I'm not asking you to forget. I'm only working on the 'let's be friends' list. Really good friends."

His boyish look rattled her. "I might concede a

little since you bought me that great lunch. Let's be friends, but it stops there.''

He pulled himself up from the desktop and rested his hands on her shoulder.

With her eyes focused on Derek, she hadn't heard anyone approach until a feminine throat-clearing caused her to turn toward the sound. From Derek's changed expression, she realized the woman had to be the infamous boss's daughter.

"Patricia," Derek said.

"I hope I'm not disturbing you."

Though Derek said no and sent her a pleasant smile, Jess heard tension constrict his voice. "I'm showing Jess the office. Patricia, Jessamy Cosette, an old friend. Jess, this is Patricia Holmes."

The woman's left eyebrow arched quizzically. "How do you do?"

"Fine thanks. It's nice to meet you." Jess arched her own eyebrow in dueling retaliation. Had their eyebrows been banjos, they might have made the top of the music charts.

Intrigued, Jess gave the woman her full attention, feeling underdressed in her gray slacks and raspberry tunic sweater. Patricia glimmered in a deep-red dress with a complementary scarf flowing beneath the wide lapels of her plunging neckline. Her tiny waist was cinched by a matching cloth belt with a gold buckle. Plain gold jewelry completed her ensemble. The woman looked good and knew it.

"Once you finish with your friend, Derek, I need to go over a few matters with you."

"Sure," he said. "In a minute. I'll catch you in your office."

Jess grimaced at Derek's words. With Patricia's obvious interest in him, the catching would be easy.

"Don't be long," she said. Turning to Jess, she gave her the twice-over before spinning on her high heels and heading toward the door. Her footsteps clicked against the tile floor, and Jess wondered how she'd missed her approach.

"Friendly," Jess said when she was out of earshot. "Nice to meet you, too," she said to the vanished woman.

"I apologize for Patricia," Derek said. "She gets that way when...when we get under pressure here. I'm sure the New York contingency is on her mind."

"I knew something was on her mind." Jess bit her tongue rather than say any more. The woman obviously didn't like competition, although Jess didn't consider herself in contention for anything...much.

Derek sent Jess an uneasy glance and flipped through a stack of papers. "We have some more details to finalize before the New York visit."

"Then...you're busy," Jess said, eyeing her watch. "I'd better get going. Don't want the boss's daughter to get her scarf in a twist."

Jess envisioned wrapping the scarf around the woman's throat and giving it a few deft jerks.

He nodded. "Right. I'd better—"

"No problem." She shot him one of his playful winks. "I'll see you at dinner."

He gave her a preoccupied nod.

Disappointed, Jess said goodbye and headed for the parking lot. From the look on Patricia's face, she could almost hear the woman giving Derek a tongue-lashing about bringing a friend to the station.

Jess reined in her irritation with the woman and paused at her car, deciding if she should drive into downtown Royal Oak before she headed back to the house. She'd heard about the new image the town had generated—boutiques, quaint shops and small cafés. She could look for a new dress. Something with a deep V-neck maybe. Fire-engine red.

Startled by her catty thoughts, Jess felt the muscles tighten in her shoulders and her headache increase. Forget Patricia, she told herself, and forget shopping. She had to keep a grip on her good sense.

Lounging in bed the next morning, Jess reviewed the situation. Reality had settled on her as gentle and unsuspecting as a satin sheet. She longed to move back home. Move her business to Michigan.

She'd wrestled with the facts over and over in her mind, fearing her unwanted attraction to Derek had motivated her idea. As foolish as it was, each time she looked at him, her heart flipped like a tiddledy-wink. But it was more than that.

In the past year her catering business had become a problem. The original effortless agreement, made a few years earlier with Louise Russell, had slowly dis-integrated into rough sandpaper.

After Jess invested into a full financial partnership, Louise balked at the change. Now Jess expected her to spend equal time planning and preparing food, but her partner had other ideas. She wanted to oversee and let assistants do the work. So Jess shouldered the major day-to-day responsibilities. And expanding had become another crux. Louise wanted no part of adding small dinner parties or dessert affairs. Every time Jess suggested a way to expand the business, Louise tossed her idea in the trash.

Jess sensed more and more that Louise would like to make a change in their partnership, and when Jess thought about it, the idea seemed reasonable—and opportune. She felt ready for change. She'd found the impetus to dissolve the partnership, but along with it, she'd uncovered a major distraction. Derek.

Swinging her legs over the edge of the bed, Jess pondered what to do. She hoped Derek had left for the studio by now. At the moment she didn't want to see him. When she did, romantic images spun through her head in a whirl, despite her common sense prodding her with warning signals.

Wisdom told her that if she were to start a new business, she needed to devote all her time and attention to the project. And Derek had new goals he was pursuing, too.

Worse, Derek was Meg's kid brother—two years younger—and a royal pain in the rear. He'd embarrassed her, tormented her, and everyone in town knew how she felt about him.

Reality poked her like a sharp stick. She'd never live down the razzing she'd receive by falling in love with the man who'd made her teen years miserable.

After she dressed, Jess wandered downstairs. Meg's voice floated from her small makeshift office, and Jess spotted her seated behind the desk, talking on the telephone. Jess took a deep breath, relieved that she'd have a few minutes alone to collect her thoughts.

Entering the kitchen, her heart dipped and punched her in the stomach. Derek sat at the kitchen table, the morning newspaper spread out in front of him. He lifted his beguiling blue eyes, and butterflies fluttered in her chest.

"Good morning," he said in a voice so tender it surprised her.

"No work today?" She grabbed a mug from the hook, sloshed in some of the fragrant coffee and slid the pot back onto the warmer. When she rotated to face him, his gaze hadn't shifted, and the look unraveled her. She gripped the mug with both hands to steady them.

"I'm working on a story. Last night we covered a police chase—a stolen car. I was assigned the story."

Watching his color heighten with his telling, Jess's own interest was piqued. She pulled out a chair and joined him. "What happened?"

"The police decided to ram the car to stop the thief, and an officer ended up in the hospital. Pretty serious condition."

"I hope he'll be okay."

"Last I heard he'll be fine. I'm interviewing his partner this morning for a follow-up report."

"I'm busy, too."

A flicker of amusement etched his face. "You're not working on a feature story, are you?"

"No." She chuckled.

"Is it business or pleasure?" Though his tone sounded nonchalant, his expression belied it.

"I need to call my partner. She's miserable working alone. I had to do some fancy negotiating to get the time away." She lowered her eyes and studied the inside of the mug. Looking anywhere but at him felt safer.

Derek folded the paper and slid it to the edge of the table, then stretched his legs out in front of him. His foot nestled against hers. She moved her foot back an inch. His followed.

"Do you like that kind of partnership?" he asked. Leaning back, he lifted his arms and knitted his hands behind his head.

Her gaze involuntarily raised to meet his. "In the beginning the situation was workable, but now...I think I'd like to buy out and do my own thing. Maybe expand." Admitting her private thoughts sent uncertainty skittering through her.

Derek lowered his arms and leaned forward on his elbows. "By doing your own thing, do you mean adding a full-blown sandwich to those bite-size nuggets?" He sent her a wry grin.

Unbidden, her gaze drifted to his inviting lips. Jess swallowed and clasped the table edge to keep from catapulting into his arms. *Stop!* She wasn't sure if her inner cry was for him or herself.

"No," she said, her pitch wavering in the ozone.

She gathered her wits and unclamped the tension in her throat. "More like small dinner parties, maybe for eight or ten at the most. Full dinners served in private homes."

"Nice idea. Better than those overrated buffets. I like small private dinner parties—like the one that I want to enjoy with you tonight. What do you say?"

Chapter Five

"Uh..." Jess's tongue stuck to the roof of her mouth.

"I'm not suggesting you cook dinner." He slid his hand across the table and captured her fingers. "I'll take care of the details."

His touch dragged her into a murky stream, and she wrestled her good sense like a hungry crocodile. Her good sense lost. "When you put it that way, how can I refuse?"

He moved his hand to her wrist, brushing her skin with a feathery caress and sending a wave of teasing emotion to every nerve in her body.

"I enjoy spending time with you, Jess," he said. "This is the way it should have been all along."

She shifted her arm away from his touch, confused at his meaning.

"Maybe one day you'll learn to trust me." His

color heightened and he chuckled. "Since you arrived, I've reverted back ten years. I'm stumbling over my own feet. Please forgive me?"

"Nothing to forgive, Derek. We both have adjustments to make. Time passed, but our memories stood still. It takes a while to catch up." She smiled at him, realizing that what she'd said made sense.

"I like that, Jess. Sounds better than thinking I'm still an idiot."

He slid his palm beneath hers and cupped his other hand above. "I have a confession, Jess. I had the worst thing for you in high school. You excited me every time I laid eyes on you."

"Don't tell me that. You're trying to embarrass me." But her thoughts flew back to Meg's words the day she arrived.

"I'm serious. I fell over myself every time I saw you. But...you were like one of the family. Always hanging around. Spending the night here in those little pajama things that rode up your leg and—"

"Please, no details. You hated me, Derek. I think your memory has me mixed up with someone else." She shook her head, but her eyes never left his.

"I'm not mixed up. Your coming back into my life is—"

"Good morning."

Meg's voice pierced the moment, and Derek shot up like a cork leaving a champagne bottle.

"Sorry, did I scare you?" his sister asked from the doorway.

"No," Jess said, positive her flustered emotion had branded a confession on her forehead.

Meg eyed her brother. "What's wrong with you, Derek? You jumped a foot."

"I just realized what time it is. If I don't get moving, I'll be late for an interview." Derek turned his back on Meg and rolled his eyes.

Jess covered her smile.

"Don't let us keep you," Meg said, grasping a cup from the hook and lifting the coffeepot.

"I'll call you later," Derek whispered to Jess as he passed. He strode from the room without looking back.

Meg filled her cup and faced Jess. "What's eating him?"

Jess fiddled with her coffee mug, pushing it one way, then turning it the other. "Nothing. I was telling him that I need to check in with my partner. Do you mind if I use the phone? I have a calling card."

"Silly. Call anyone you want—and no calling card. Derek can afford the bill." She took a sip of the strong brew and her face darkened. "Problems?"

Tension skittered down Jess's back. Had she heard their conversation? "What?"

"Problems…with your partner? You said you had to call her." She set the mug on the table and rested her chin in her hand.

Jess's shoulders relaxed. "No problems, really. I'm worried she's committed hara-kiri. Louise hates running the place alone."

"Ah," Meg said, sending her a comforting smile. "I'm sorry. That must be a pain."

Jess nodded, her heart warmed by Meg's concern. But to her dismay, what warmed her more was Derek's dinner invitation.

Derek held the receiver with his fingers clenched tightly around it. He despised disappointing Jess, but that was what he had to do. He heard the first ring, then the second. What would he do if Jess wasn't home?

"Randolph residence."

Jess's voice sailed through the line.

"Hi. This is Derek." He closed his eyes, trying to find the right words.

She chuckled, and the sound dislodged his tethered guilt like a clog in the bathroom drain. Gummy and unpleasant.

"I recognized your voice," she said.

He opened his mouth and found only silence.

"Is something wrong?" she asked.

"I'm really sorry, Jess. I have to disappoint you."

"Disappoint me?"

He'd spent his life being a disappointment to her, calling her childish names, embarrassing her, acting like a... Derek let the word drop. "I ran into a problem with a special report I've been working on. Tonight's the only night I can tape the interviews." Thinking back, Derek realized he'd done everything for his career. That had been all he wanted. Now the only thing he knew he wanted for sure was Jess.

"That's your job, Derek. You have more to think about than me, especially with the anchor position in sight."

"Thanks for understanding."

"Anything serious?"

"Another baby kidnapping, this one out of the hospital, if you can believe it. I suggested we do a story on hospital security. We're filming two interviews tonight." He paused, thinking of the drama he witnessed daily.

"Sad stuff. I don't envy you."

"I'll make it up to you," Derek said. "We'll have dinner another evening." Another evening? When? His time always seemed schedule-locked. "Next time nothing will get in my way." Derek could only imagine what Jess was thinking.

"Don't apologize, Derek."

"Thanks," he said. "This is one of the difficult things about my job. Like last night, I spent a couple of hours taking notes before going to sleep...." Notes? He'd forgotten them. "Rats. I left the folder home on my desk." He rubbed his aching eyes. "And I really need it."

"When?" Jess asked.

"Tonight. I don't suppose..." He stumbled over his question. How could he cancel the dinner plans and then ask her to bring him the folder? He scrutinized the work in front of him. "You don't happen to be... Never mind, I'll have to... Here's an idea. Is Meg there?"

"She's not here, and is all that hemming and hawing an attempt to ask me for a favor?'' A sliver of humor drifted through the wire.

''No...yes, I suppose it is.''

''Just ask me, Derek. Maybe you'd like me to drop the folder off at the studio?''

''Only if you're going out.'' Please be going out, he thought.

''It so happens,'' she said, ''I'm having lunch with a couple of friends at the deli near your office. I can drop it off in an hour or so. Will that work?''

''More than work, Jess. It'd be perfect.''

''I'll see you then,'' she said. ''But remember— you owe me. And big.''

Her teasing voice played in his head. He replaced the receiver on the cradle and sat for a moment, reviewing the past couple of days with Jess. She'd sent his emotions on a wild ride. A ride that felt as if it would change his life.

Jess pulled away from the curb, her thoughts heading in a hundred directions. She didn't mind doing Derek a favor. She'd be pleased to do it if...if what? What did she expect? She had no idea. Events had thrown her into a tizzy.

Maybe the nostalgia of the past two days had set her in a rare mood—like an old late-night movie. The heroine stands on the brink of a cliff, the wind pounding against her back, her life empty, the swirling waters below beckoning. Then out of the mist, a handsome hero rushes to her side and clasps her to him. They gaze into each other's eyes, and all animosity vanishes in the haze. He lavishes her with kisses and promises her love everlasting. The end.

Jess cringed at her musings. She'd never been a romantic. So why now? And why Derek? Neither of them was in a position to save each other from anything. In terms of career, they seemed to be in the same spot. Uncertain. His dream was climbing the ladder of success, and she had her dreams to pursue, too. Although at this point, she didn't know whether her career ladder was leading her up or down.

Jess spied the deli and parked. She grabbed the folder and hurried down the block toward the studio. At the intersection, a cool breeze whipped around the corner of a building, and Jess's autumn jacket didn't hold back the cold.

She waited, her thoughts drifting to Louise. She needed to call her again in a couple of days. During their conversation earlier in the day, panic had riddled her partner's voice. Maybe now was a good time to broach the subject of severing the partnership. Then again, would Jess be severing her jugular vein at the same time?

When the light changed, Jess crossed the street, and as she stepped into the studio's shadow, the chill deepened. She hoped this wasn't some kind of omen.

She flinched at her thought. Omen? She'd never believed in omens. For the past three days, she'd been as addled as a sheep without a shepherd. One moment she headed in one direction. The next minute she went the other way. Her thoughts. Her plans. Her emotions.

She tugged open the door, marched through the

lobby and waited for the elevator. Why had she allowed Derek to rile her so? She felt like a puppet with no puppeteer. No. That was wrong. Derek was the puppeteer.

Her heart yo-yoed as the elevator came to a halt. She exited and headed down the corridor, hoping she'd find Derek without any trouble. When she peeked into the large newsroom, she could see him through the glass of the smaller office.

Rather than waltz past the newsmen, she retraced her steps and reached his office through the outside door. Before barging in, she gave a tap and waited.

"Come in," Derek called.

When she did, she saw Derek sitting at the desk while Patricia sat on it. Disappointment tumbled to Jess's toes.

Derek rose to greet her, a warm smile lighting his face. "Jess. Thanks a million. I've been so tied up here I hated to take time to drive back home. You saved the day."

"I'm glad I could help," Jess said, wondering if she really was. She handed him the folder and backed toward the door. "I know you're busy, so I won't keep you."

A rap sounded against the window, drawing Jess's attention. A man stood outside the office beckoning to Patricia. She checked her watch and slid off the desk. "Excuse me. But I have work to do." She sashayed across the small office and swung through the doorway. The door slammed behind her.

Nudged by unwanted wariness, Jess took a step back. "I'll go, too."

"Don't rush. Have a seat." He patted the chair beside his desk.

"But I thought—"

"I can spare a minute."

His appreciative look sent her on another yo-yo ride without an elevator. She wanted to ask about Patricia, but instead, she sank to the chair and folded her hands in her lap. "I only have a minute, anyway. I'm meeting Janet Pardo and Bobbi Kelly for lunch. You remember them?"

"I remember Janet. Who's Bobby?"

A frown crinkled his forehead and she laughed to herself as she realized he thought Bobbi was a man. "Roberta Kelly. We call her Bobbi."

"Roberta. Right. I remember."

He rested his elbows on his knees and leaned nearer. "Listen, Jess, I—"

"Derek."

Jess's head pivoted with the speed of light. Standing in the doorway, she saw a well-dressed, older man with graying hair and intense eyes. His presence was commanding.

"Mr. Holmes," Derek said, rising. "I'd like you to meet an old high-school friend, Jessamy Cosette." He reached for Jess's arm as she rose and shifted her forward. "This is the station owner, Jess."

"Gerald Holmes," he said, extending his hand. "I'm pleased to meet you."

"Same here. Derek's spoken highly of you." Jess

gave him a firm handshake. Studying the man, she remembered Derek's earlier comments about his boss being a family man. A man who valued marriage. A crazy thought shuffled through her head. Maybe she could give Derek a hand.

Holmes tilted back on his heels and folded his arms across his chest, his gaze on Derek. "You're working on an interview?"

"Interview?" Derek asked. In a flash his quizzical look cleared. "For the centennial spots, you mean. No, but that's not a bad idea. Jess was her senior class president."

"Sounds like an interview to me," Holmes said.

With their conversation in the background, the creative idea swept over Jess. Her plan could benefit Derek and possibly her own career. If her plans came to fruition, she'd own a catering business in town. Connections were what she needed. A TV interview might help put her name and face before the community. Holmes owned a major television studio. Making the right impression on him couldn't hurt her, either.

"Do you live in town?"

Jess pulled out of her thoughts and tuned into Holmes's question.

"No, I'm visiting. I have a pretty successful catering business in Cincinnati." She took a lengthy breath and let her scheme surface. "But Derek and I have been...good friends for a long time, and when he invited me back home for the centennial—" she slid her arm around Derek's waist and felt him tense

"—he suggested we might do some celebrating of our own."

Tilting back on his heels again, Holmes smiled. "Well, now, that sounds promising." He gripped Derek's shoulder and gave it a good-old-boy shake. "I'm pleased. Very pleased." He paused a moment and stroked his chin. "But that doesn't preclude an interview if you're willing." He peered at Jess.

"An interview would be nice," she said, sensing her idea had hit its mark in both directions.

Holmes's face brightened again. "Derek, maybe you could set something up. 'Hometown girl makes good' is always a great feature story."

Derek rubbed the back of his neck. "I'll work something up, sir."

"Good, and Jess, I hope we have some time to get to know each other." He gave Derek a wink. "Maybe over dinner one evening."

"Sounds good, sir," Derek said.

Holmes sent Jess a knowing look and strode away.

Afraid to speak, she waited for Derek's response to her ploy.

"So that's the boss," she said finally to break the strained silence.

Derek's face mottled. "Jess, what made you do that? He thinks that you and I are—"

"Serious," she said. "Isn't that what you wanted?"

"Right, but…"

"But what? Now he sees you as a man broaching

marriage. At least, a relationship. You're dependable. Stable. All those good things.''

''Thanks, but what do I do when you leave and don't come back?''

She'd thought Derek would be pleased, but seeing his panic, she suspected she'd made a mistake. "Let's pretend, Derek. Take it one step at a time.''

''One step at a time? A relationship begins like that, doesn't it?''

She didn't understand his analogy and sensed he thought she'd stepped out of line. ''I'm sorry, Derek. I was only trying to help.''

''Don't be sorry.'' A mischievous smile lit his face. ''I love the idea the more I think of it. Sure. Why not pretend...'' He sidled next to her and slipped his arm around her shoulders.

''Don't love it too much,'' Jess said, pulling away.

''Be careful how you react, Jess. Holmes might be watching.'' He tilted his head toward the broad window.

Concerned that she'd already blown her hoax, she scanned the newsroom through the glass, but Holmes was nowhere in sight. More of Derek's games. She pivoted toward him and narrowed her eyes.

Derek raised his hand and caressed her cheek. ''I appreciate what you did. You were thinking of my promotion.''

Feeling a sensation wavering in her belly, she removed his hand from her face. ''Yes, and that's all. So don't get carried away.''

''You carry me away. I can't help myself.''

His line slithered through her. Was he playing games like in the old days? Teasing and taunting? Looking into his mesmerizing eyes, her pulse soared, and she tore herself from his gaze. "I have to go. The girls are waiting."

"Girls? It's been ten years. You're all women now," he said, his expression saying more than his words. He caught her hand and drew her toward him. "No kiss goodbye?"

"What are you talking about?" she whispered.

"You started this. We're a couple now, remember? And you said it yourself, we have some celebrating to do."

"I did you a favor back there and that's all." She backed toward the door. But she faltered, though desire drew her forward like a moth to a flame. The charade had turned on her.

Derek stepped nearer and rested his hands on her shoulders, drawing her closer. He tilted his head toward the window. "Like I said, Holmes might be watching."

His mouth lowered to hers, and dreamlike, she brought up her arms to encircle his neck. As gentle as spring rain, his lips caressed hers, warm and refreshing, but thunder rose in her ears and lightning charged down her limbs, electrifying her senses.

In a heartbeat Derek eased away, and without looking at his face, Jess pulled from his arms and hurried out the doorway, fighting the desire to be struck again by one more bolt of lightning.

Chapter Six

Stepping into the deli, Jess calmed herself, the kiss surging through her mind. She touched her cheek, fearing she glowed with heat, and scanned the crowd. She hadn't seen her friends since she'd gone off to college. When her gaze fell on two women in earnest conversation at a back table, Jess knew she'd found them.

She garnered her courage and approached the table. "Hi."

"Jess!" the two squealed in unison.

Nearby patrons shot questioning looks their way, and Jess felt giddy as a schoolgirl as she settled at the table. "It's been a long time."

"You look wonderful, Jess," Janet said. "You were pretty in school, but maturity has been generous. You're a beautiful woman."

"Thanks for the exaggeration," Jess said, eyeing

her two friends who hadn't fared badly, either. "Both of you look radiant."

"After two kids—two daughters—I thank you," Bobbi said.

"I have three." Janet lifted her hand into the air and spread three fingers. "Two boys and a girl."

"You've been busy," Jess said, feeling a smidgen of envy.

"So," Janet said, propping her chin on her elbows and hunching forward, "tell us about him."

"Him?"

Bobbi let loose a rousing sputter. "Derek!"

"Derek?" Jess felt the heat rise up her neck and formed her face into a scowl. "Nothing to tell."

"But you're staying with him. I can't believe it," Janet said, her eyes wide and questioning.

"I'm staying with Meg," Jess countered as her thoughts flew back to his office and his tender lips.

"I remember how much you hated him, Jess." Bobbi grinned, then picked up her menu. "The special looks good." She peeked from behind the placard. "And so does Derek—now that he's all grown up."

"He's different than he was," Jess said, surprised at her defense. "We all are."

Bobbi raised her eyebrows and sent Jess a wily smile. "But Derek has really changed. He's a hunk."

"So what's he like now that he's a TV star?" Janet asked.

Jess contained her emotional frustration and feared the truth flashed on her face like a neon sign. "He's very nice, and he's not a star. He's a reporter.'' She dropped against the chair back. "Look, is this all we're going to talk about?"

The two women looked at each other, their grins suspect. "Can you think of anything better?" Bobbi asked.

"Yes, I can." Jess grabbed the menu and tried to focus on it.

"So we'll shut up if you tell us what he's like in bed," Janet whispered.

Jess's head jerked up from behind the cardboard. "In bed?"

"Shush!" Janet warned, glancing at the nearby patrons. "This isn't a public announcement. Bobbi and I are just curious."

"Come on, Jess," Janet begged. "We're having a difficult time imagining you and Derek even speaking, let alone…"

Jess grappled with her response, then gripped the table edge and narrowed her eyes. "Ladies, you two have been my friends forever, but it's about to end."

Their faces sank.

Struggling to gather her bewildering thoughts, Jess prayed for a firm, convincing voice. "First," she said, "I'm staying with Meg, not Derek, as I've already said. Second, I'm not sleeping with Derek. Third, I have no plans to sleep with him." A soft pulsation started in her midsection and snaked its way through her limbs. In truth, she had no plans, but the possibility unsettled her, nearly depleting her of breath.

Jess refocused on her friends. "So can we talk about something else? Tell me about your kids."

Two faces grinned back at her, and she watched both women dive for their purses. In a heartbeat, two wallets flagged in Jess's face while she dragged her attention to five smiling children.

Her distraction had worked, but her heart was sinking. How many more old friends had heard she was staying with Derek? How many more questions and comments about the past would she have to endure? And worse, how would she cope with her growing desire for the man?

Derek stared at the notebook on his desk, his pencil posed and his mind blank. He'd done hundreds of interviews, hundreds of special reports, but somehow he couldn't think of how to handle Jess's TV spot. Holmes had initiated it, and Derek had no thought of telling his boss he couldn't handle the job.

Whenever he pictured her beside him in front of the cameras, his mind drifted to their brief, but pleasurable kiss, or the night Jess sat across the table from him in her robe and slippers. The event lay in his mind like snow on Christmas Day. Soft, nostalgic and beautiful.

If he'd let his passion have its way, Jess would distrust him forever. Since her arrival, she'd softened toward him, and their kiss had affirmed it. She hadn't pushed him away but had wrapped her arms around him. The remembrance slid through his belly like satin.

He felt certain she cared about him, but what he also wanted was her trust. He'd played games with her years ago. Not now. He'd put away his games. He wanted the real thing. Jess.

He stared at the paper again—more doodles than words. The interview could be one of his centennial's best. Jess sparkled with personality, she'd found success, and her beauty wasn't only in his eyes. He'd seen the way his co-workers gawked at her when he'd brought her in to see the studio.

Thinking of his co-workers, Derek looked through the window and spied a fellow reporter. He beckoned to him, and Jim signaled he'd come in a minute.

Derek knew what he wanted to accomplish during Jess's interview. He would show her talent, her charm, her business sense and her success. But what else? Could he learn something he didn't already know?

"Hey," Jim said, slipping through the doorway. "Why are you holed up in here?"

"I'm stuck on an interview."

"You? Mr. Dazzle? I've never seen you at a loss for words." Jim pulled up a chair, swung it around and straddled it, then rested his chin on his hands. "What's eating you?"

Derek shook his head. "She's a friend. I'm too close. You know—I can't see the forest for the trees."

"Too close?" His brows shot up. "How close?"

"Not that close." Derek said the words, but his evasion slithered up his neck. He prayed it would stay undetected.

"Wouldn't happen to be that babe you had here the other day, would it?"

Derek nodded. "Okay, I like her. A lot. But just get me started."

Jim grinned and turned as if facing a television camera. "Today, I have Miss Sexy Lady with me who graduated—"

"Jessamy Cosette," Derek supplied.

Jim smiled. "Just let the viewer know who she was then and who she is now." He turned back to the camera. "Tell me about high school, Jessamy. Any special memories?" Jim slapped his leg. "Maybe that's what you're afraid of, Derek. Does she have special memories of you?"

"Thanks, Jim. My mind's working again. I can take it from here."

Jim rose and clapped Derek on the back. "Knew I could help you." He chuckled as he opened the door and left.

Derek stared down at the paper. What he really wanted to know was whether or not Jess would consider moving back to Royal Oak. She'd talked about splitting from her partner. Why not bring the business to Michigan?

Looking forward to scouting out downtown Royal Oak, Jess made her way to Center Street. She parked, then walked over to Washington and wandered from shop to boutique admiring the clothing, the glitzy jewelry and unique gifts.

Since she hadn't packed for many dressy events,

Jess stepped into a clothing store and found two after-five dresses. Unable to choose between them, she purchased them both, then returned to her car and drove the short distance to Derek's.

Juggling her packages, she let herself in, but before she passed the kitchen, Meg whipped through the doorway.

"You're late. Where have you been?"

"Shopping." Jess lifted her packages. "Drove through Royal Oak and decided to meander a bit. Plus, I felt compelled to boost the local economy."

"I wondered what had happened to you."

"You know me. The dress shop held me up. When I thought of the parties and dances coming up, I realized I hadn't brought the right clothes." She grinned. "Sounds like a good excuse, anyway."

"Who needs an excuse?" Meg pulled back the edge of one of Jess's shopping bags and peeked inside. "So let's see what you bought."

Jess motioned to her. "Come up, and I'll hang these things while I show you."

Jess handed Meg one of the large shopping bags and beckoned her up the stairs. In her room, Jess dropped the packages on the bed and pulled her purchases from their wrappings.

"Nice," Meg said, feeling the cloth. "Really unique. Looks like something from the forties."

"It is, I think. I bought it at Patti Smith's Collectibles."

As Jess displayed her garments, Meg oohed and

ahhed, offering fashion suggestions the way she always did.

"I love that shimmering amber number, too," Meg said. "Add gold evening shoes and the right jewelry, and you could knock some guy's socks off without even trying."

Jess grinned, then hung up her new outfits, thinking that the next time she ran into Miss Arched Eyebrow, she'd show her a thing or two. Startled by her aggressiveness, she drew a deep breath and expelled it with a loud blast.

Meg's brow wrinkled and a curious look glided across her face. "Something wrong?"

"No. I'm just tired."

"Then this is a good night to relax. I just put dinner in the oven, and…" Meg clasped her hands together. "I have a great idea. How about going on a treasure hunt with me in the attic? I'm on the decorating committee for the centennial, and I have to find old yearbooks and school memorabilia."

"Before dinner?" Jess asked, thinking she'd rather put her feet up or soak in the tub.

"Sure. It'll be fun. We've got a good hour."

"Okay. You're on." Jess hated to disappoint her friend.

She trudged up the narrow staircase behind Meg. At the top of the stairs, Jess peered into the shadows. The late-afternoon sun, glinting through the small, round window, painted a cockeyed circle on the dusty floor. Dust fairies skittered along as she made her way to a corner where Meg tugged on a string dangling from the ceiling. A bare, soiled lightbulb sent off a meek glow.

Two old sleeping bags stretched along the bare wood floor, and Meg tugged a few cardboard boxes over to them and sat. She tugged open one of the boxes.

Jess opened another, gazing at the out-of-style clothing she pulled from the carton.

Meg winced, eyeing a short plaid skirt. "I can't believe we still have all this trash up here. We should have a masquerade party."

Ogling the garments, Meg and Jess tugged items from the box—a polyester leisure suit, madras shirt and a suede Indian-beaded vest.

"I think I wore this in fifth grade," Meg said, stroking the suede. "Wonder if it still fits?" She laughed.

A sound filtered through their chuckles as footsteps trudged up the attic stairs. Jess watched the opening until Derek's head appeared, followed by his broad shoulders and long, solid legs.

"A trip into the past?" He ambled across the planking toward them. "You ladies have nothing better to do?" His gaze caught Jess's as she sprawled on the sleeping bag.

"We're looking for high-school stuff," Meg said.

"Decorations for the dance," Jess explained, hoping her voice sounded natural.

"Let me help." Derek flipped open one of the cartons. He dug inside until he pulled out a football jersey and Meg's school sweater. "Look what I found."

"Those ought to be good for a laugh," Meg said.

Derek eyed the jersey. "Seems like an eternity since I wore this thing."

"It has been," Jess said. As she admired his handsome face, any taunts shriveled away. Gratefully, she knew the terrible memories had begun to fade.

Derek eyed her with a look of surprise. "Nothing else? No barbs?" He dropped the jersey into the open box and gave Jess a relieved smile.

"I think this is where I came in," Meg said, rising and brushing the dirt from her pant legs.

"Don't run away, Meg," Jess said. "You haven't heard either of us make one dig or hateful comment. Share the rare moment." She grinned at Derek.

Meg shook her head. "Why don't you two look for the yearbooks while I check dinner?" Meg stepped toward the staircase, then paused to look at her watch. "It'll be about twenty minutes. Okay?"

"Okay," Derek said.

Apprehensive, Jess wondered if she should follow Meg downstairs and recommend they search later, but Meg had already vanished and Derek appeared at her side with two more cartons from the corner.

He sank beside her on the sleeping bag with a grin. "Finally. We're alone."

Chapter Seven

"If you don't behave, you'll be totally alone," Jess said.

Derek gave her a wink, then turned to open another box. The fragrance of his aftershave washed over her. She watched him roll up his shirtsleeves and delve inside, and her memory flew back years, recalling Derek's large youthful hands catching a spiraling football pass. As much as he irked her, even then she'd admired his strong, tapered fingers, but she never would have told him.

The whole attic brought back a wave of memories. This was the spot she and Meg had experimented with cigarettes and where they hid from Derek when they wanted to be alone to discuss their first romantic kisses.

Pushing her discomfort aside, Jess peered into a

newly opened box and seeing the contents, let out a cheer.

Derek glanced her way. "Yearbooks?"

She nodded and grabbed one. The date on the cover carried her back eleven years. She flipped through the pages, finding her eleventh-grade class photo.

"Look," she said, pointing.

Derek leaned down and eyed it with a chuckle. "No wonder I called you String Bean. You're as straight as a pole. Not a bump on you anywhere."

"I've matured, remember?" she said, aware of his taunting grin.

Revenge slithered through her, and before digging out another yearbook, she located a candid shot of Derek and propped the annual on his knees. "String Bean, huh? Wait until you see this." The annual teetered from its perch and slid to the bedroll.

As if prearranged, together they stretched out on the sleeping bags and propped themselves on their elbows.

"You thought I looked bad." She gave him a playful smirk. "Look at you." Jess poked the picture with her index finger. Enjoying Derek's squirming humiliation, Jess aimed his attention to the baby-fat paunch stretching his T-shirt and bulging slightly over his jean's belt.

"I was pitiful," Derek muttered, rolling onto his back and gaping at the picture. "Thank the good Lord, I learned about exercise and realized greens weren't only for rabbits." He rolled back and threw an arm over her shoulders. "You and I made a great couple, didn't we, Jess? You with too little and me with too much.''

With her sweater tangled beneath her, she watched Derek focus on the knitted cloth pulling against her breasts and linger there before shifting back to her face. He drew his palm over her cheek and cupped her chin in his hand. Beneath his tender touch, heat pumped through Jess's veins.

She wasn't alone. Derek appeared to struggle with the mounting emotion, too. Then he rolled to his side and slid his arm around her waist, drawing her against him. His look softened, and his gaze glided down her neck to her breasts. Mesmerized, Jess felt his hand caress her back in tender circles, and she trembled.

When his lips parted as if to speak—to ask—Jess gave him her answer by yielding her mouth to his. Their lips touched like the strike of a match—sparks, fire and heat. She felt herself drowning in a swirling, liquid blaze. Moving, undulating, melting.

Emotion rippled through her body and her moan united with his. Tenderly he released her, their gazes still locked in eager surprise.

Neither spoke. Then he shifted his hand, moving it along her arm and touching the underside of her forearm. His fingers moved against the side of her breast, and she drew a breath and held it.

He stopped, his eyes questioning. Surprised by her rising passion, Jess eased away. Without a word, he understood and respected her wishes.

Instead, he lowered his mouth to hers again while he stroked her jaw and caressed her heated cheek. The edge of his tongue brushed against her upper lip, and a deep ache rose in her belly.

Fighting her desire, Jess prodded herself to inch back, as Meg's voice funneled up the staircase and halted them. "Hey you two, dinner's ready."

Like children playing doctor, Jess and Derek jumped apart, adjusting clothing and hiding guilt-laden faces. The sudden awareness of what they were doing burst her ballooning desire into embarrassed laughter.

"What's so funny?" Meg called.

"Old yearbooks," Jess answered, her voice sounding throaty and strange in her ear.

Derek rose from their floor bed and offered her a hand. Standing against him, she felt his uneven breathing matching her own.

"Are you coming?" Meg called.

Her question brought self-conscious titters as they hustled to gather their wits and move toward the staircase.

Jess gave Derek an urgent poke. "I lost my head for a minute, Derek. But you know this is foolish. It can't happen again."

Her words were as much for herself as for him. But Jess knew she'd have to use more than the words to protect her heart. She needed to cover herself with a coat of armor to shield herself from Derek's relentless charm.

Jess struggled through dinner, trying not to look Derek directly in the eye. They ate in silence while

Meg rattled on about her latest novel plot. But a lull in the conversation triggered her awareness. Meg dropped her fork, which clattered against the plate, and gawked at them. "What's up?"

Like remorseful children, neither spoke.

"You look guilty as sin." Her head pivoted like a tennis spectator. "What happened in the attic?" She narrowed her eyes.

Jess's mouth fell open, but not so much in surprise as in embarrassment. "Heavens, Meg, what do you mean?"

Derek leaned back in the chair. "I think we have a bit more class than to fool around in the attic. Don't you, Meg?" A faint tinge of mottled color rose on his neck, but he held his ground and gazed calmly at his sister.

"Well, I don't know. Both of you look as if you've been up to something." Meg paused, clearly disconcerted.

Jess grappled for any acceptable response. "I'm just tired, Meg. It's been a busy day...and you know how it is in a strange place. Some nights a person can't sleep."

Jess forked a bite of food into her mouth, then challenged her throat to swallow. The forkful slid downward leaving a lump in her chest. "That's all it is."

Jess's reaction touched her like a match. Why did she feel apologetic and embarrassed? Because it was Derek. Would her growing feelings always be dampened by their past?

Wanting to smooth the tension, Jess skewered another piece of chicken and changed the subject to a safer topic. "How long will you stay in Royal Oak, Meg? Any plans?"

"Until I can't bear it anymore, I suppose. Home is where the heart is, but excitement is usually somewhere else."

Home. Again the word rolled through Jess's chest. Though Cincinnati had been good for her career, the city where she had been raised nestled warm and comfortable in her thoughts. "I imagine it's boring here after living in New York."

"Quieter, but New York can get tedious," Meg said. "You can't drive in the city if you value your life…or your wallet. Parking prices are atrocious, so that means traveling by taxis and subways."

"Sounds good to me," Derek said. "I'd give my SUV for a job in New York." He sidled a look toward Jess.

Hearing his words, Jess's stomach somersaulted. Had New York been part of Derek's plan all along? The New Yorkers' visit to the television station now took a whole new turn. She studied Derek's face without success. With her stomach doing acrobatics with her dinner, she pushed her food around on her plate and refocused on Meg.

"Any handsome man in the wings?" Jess asked, and after seeing Meg's expression, wished she hadn't.

Looking into the distance, Meg didn't answer immediately. When she did, she sounded thoughtful. "Maybe someday. Jack wasn't a bad guy. We just made each other miserable. We were on two different ocean liners heading to opposite ports. Our interests drifted.''

Derek let out a telling groan.

Meg's eyes narrowed, and she shot Derek a look that a person could aim only at a sibling.

"Sorry, Meg. It was the 'drifting interests,'" Derek said with a look of sincere apology.

The cryptic interaction between brother and sister piqued Jess's curiosity, and she looked from Meg to Derek waiting for some kind of explanation.

Meg's shoulders slumped and she turned to Jess. "You may as well know. Jack had an affair." She glared at Derek. "There, I said it." She swung back to Jess. "Our interests 'drifted' is a nice way to say mine turned to writing, and Jack's to another woman. I'm sorry I didn't tell you earlier."

Jess's bewilderment shifted to compassion. "I'm sorry, Meg. I didn't know. If a man had you to love, I can't believe he'd look at another woman. I always envied you."

Meg's eyes widened. "Me? Why?"

"You were always so perfect." Jess's confession felt strange, but looking at Meg's face, she knew her friend could use some bolstering. "Pretty. Great shape. Spunky. You have beautiful red hair. I admired your clothes. You seemed to have a knack for putting things together. I always felt like a rag bag next to you."

Derek chuckled. "Rag bag? That's because you had no shape."

"Thanks, Derek, for another trip down memory

lane. Will you ever grow up?'' She shook her fork at him. ''Do you have to make a joke out of everything?''

His grin faded. ''I'm teasing, Jess. I thought I'd lighten the moment.'' Dodging the fork, he brought her hand to his lips.

Jess jerked away. ''Don't try to sweet-talk me. You have no sensitivity to anyone's feelings. You're still the same idiot you used to be.''

As soon as the words were out, Jess's heart sank. Why had she attacked Derek? Was she so afraid of being attracted to him that she had to destroy him? She knew she should say she was sorry, but the words stuck in her throat.

The room hung heavy with silence. Derek stared at his plate for an uncomfortable few moments before he spoke. ''First of all, Jess, I really did just want to lighten the moment. But now I want you—both of you—to listen.''

A frown marred his face and his eyes darkened. ''Do the two of you think I didn't have any problems in high school? You think big lumbering teenage males are so blasted self-assured. Well, you don't know anything. Those pictures of me in the yearbook were a horrible reminder. Neither of you have any idea.''

Startled, Jess glanced at Meg, then focused on Derek.

''And you both know how much football meant to me. Can you imagine how I felt when I didn't play well enough for a pro bid like some of my friends?

Instead, I turned to broadcasting. I worked hard to make something of myself, and I'm tired of being reminded what a jerk I was." He bolted from the chair, plunked his plate in the sink and left the room.

Through a blur of tears, Jess saw Meg's mouth gape as she watched Derek stride through the doorway.

"What happened?" Meg asked.

"Obviously it was what I said." Jess's head was spinning. "Who would have thought?"

"Not me," Meg said, staring across the room, her mind obviously stretching back in time.

Jess's mind followed. Derek had strutted around her like a rooster in a barnyard. She'd never imagined he lacked anything but manners. And from his reaction today, whatever bothered him years ago hadn't been resolved.

Derek stood in his bedroom, wondering why he'd acted so rashly. He'd started the whole thing—poking at Jess with his stupid "no shape" comments, just as he had when they were kids. But they weren't kids anymore. He was falling in love with her all over again.

To make matters worse, he'd blurted out the self-doubt he'd kept buried for so many years. He chided himself. How many teens didn't act like buffoons to cover the fear of rejection and competition?

He recalled his newfound hormones jangling in high school. Like his buddies, he'd stay seated or stand with his books clamped low in front of him—

anything to hide the telltale excitement caused by a pretty girl's smile.

Especially a pretty girl like Jess. Though thinking back, he'd seen Jess aim very few smiles at him.

Strange being an adult and still feeling the pangs of his teen years. Yet those were the days that cut the notches in his sexuality. He'd grown too fast and by thirteen, was tripping over his size-twelve shoes. Though his height made him appear older, his chubby waistline and hairless chest did little to give him confidence. Football had saved the day.

The coach wanted big, lumbering head-butters. And he was good at that. And the bonus was that every girl in school—or almost every girl—wanted to date a football player. So he blundered his clumsy way through idiotic dates: movies, hamburgers, first-date feels in the back seat of a car and second-date positions he could write a book about. But he knew they weren't really after him, only his varsity jacket.

Derek thanked God that by his first year of college he'd begun to change. His waist trimmed down and his chest hair grew. And even though he had failed in football, he'd survived and regained self-confidence, as well as learned a few social graces.

Still, remnants of his old ways clung to him like static cling. Beginning his first big job at Channel 5, he'd allowed Patricia to lead him around by the nose, but as time passed, he reclaimed his confidence, though Patricia wielded her threat on occasion, suggesting she could get him booted out if she talked to Daddy.

But Derek ignored her. Holmes assigned him quality feature stories, and he'd gained media stature and respect from his boss.

So what was wrong? Since Jess's visit, things had changed. Whenever Derek spotted himself in a mirror, an overweight, obnoxious teenager looked back at him. Who would think a polished, educated, experienced television newscaster would be jolted by self-doubt?

Angry at himself, he stared at the bedroom floor and kicked yesterday's briefs beneath the bed. In retaliation, he snatched them from the carpet and dropped them into the hamper. But he wasn't a kid anymore. Kicking and hiding didn't solve the problem. Apologizing to Jess might help. He sat on the edge of the bed, mentally writing his script and rehearsing his lines the way he did for each news feature.

When he'd gathered his thoughts, he strode from his inner sanctum and into the living room. Jess and Meg were talking softly, but when he entered the room, their conversation died.

He apologized softly. "Sorry. I overreacted to what you said."

"We were surprised," Meg said.

Looking at Jess's face, Derek figured she understood. "I guess I was angry at myself."

He stood at the far end of the sofa while Jess curled in the corner of the other end. "Teenage girls seem to have more natural self-esteem than guys," Derek said, giving Jess what he hoped was a playful grin.

"Forget it, Derek." She returned his smile. "I should apologize to you." Jess patted the empty sofa cushion beside her, and with the darker mood broken, Derek accepted the invitation.

The women's conversation took up where they'd left off earlier, and as Derek watched Jess, looking so familiar and so beautiful, he wondered how she could have envied Meg years ago.

Admiring her in silence, Derek relaxed. In a brighter mood, Jess seemed more like the person he'd met on the freeway—or the friend who'd shared his middle-of-the-night breakfast.

Images of her settled in his mind. The pretty teenager grown into a gorgeous woman. He wondered how it would feel to share all his meals with her.

Sitting beneath the studio lights, Derek felt beads of perspiration forming along his hairline. Or was that an excuse? He turned from the camera and faced Jess. "Thanks, Jessamy Cosette. Your hometown congratulates you on your successful career."

Derek shifted to face the television camera. "Stay tuned to Channel 5 as we welcome more Royal Oak High School alumni during the upcoming centennial celebration."

"That's it," a voice said from behind the lights.

Relieved, Jess let out a puff of constrained air. "It's over?"

"It's a wrap," Derek said, his own shoulders relaxing. "You did good, Jessamy Cosette. You'll have the viewers eating out of your hands—just like me."

His face shifted to a silly smile. "Now if we're talking about those hors d'oeuvres, I should say they'll be eating out of *their* hands."

She grinned and rose. "Thanks. Can we get out from under these hot lights?"

"Wait over there, and I'll be finished in a minute." He motioned away from the lights, then stepped away to talk with the cameraman.

Jess wandered to the side and looked around the studio. Under the lights, she had seen very little, but now, she could see Holmes talking to someone in the control booth.

She thought the interview had gone well. Derek had rehearsed his questions with her before the taping, and with his glib, easy manner, she'd actually enjoyed herself.

During the show, he'd asked her about moving the catering business to the area. Not wanting to let him know she'd already begun to make plans, she'd only hinted that it might be possible. She'd been surprised he'd asked the question.

Casting a sidelong glance at the control booth, she could almost see a sparkle in Gerald Holmes's eye as he awarded his stamp of approval on the "as good as married" Derek.

Derek had warned her that Holmes would probably drop by to watch part of the taping, so she'd been prepared. During the interview, she tried to balance her behavior between successful businesswoman and woman in love with the reporter. The ploy wasn't easy—not since she'd lost the ability to tell the difference between a ruse and the real thing.

"Good job," Holmes said.

Not hearing his approach, Jess jumped. "Thanks."

"I thought you might like to join us for dinner on Friday. It's my thank-you to Derek for his hard work, and it will give me a chance to get to know you better." He sent her a knowing smile. "Just in case something serious should happen between the two of you."

"You never know," Jess said, offering him her best coy smile. "And I'd love to join you."

"Wonderful."

"What's wonderful?" Derek asked as he appeared at Jess's side.

"Fine job, Derek, as always," Holmes said, giving his shoulder a pat. "I figured I'd invite your young lady to our little dinner party."

"Invite Jess?" A frown bounced onto his face. "I thought it was our last meeting before the New York visitors arrive."

Holmes folded his arms and rocked back on his heels. "Our business will be brief, and really, I'd like to get to know this young lady a little better." He unwrapped his arms and rested a hand on Jess's shoulder.

Looking at Derek's face, Jess knew something was wrong, and if he wasn't careful, he'd make Holmes suspicious about their charade.

"That would be great, but...I have a meeting with the taping crew on Friday before dinner, and I agreed to drive Patricia to the restaurant.'' He slid his hand into his trouser pocket and plucked at his car keys. ''Unless you could—''

Holmes held up his hand. ''No problem, Derek. I'd be happy to be this lovely woman's escort. You go to the meeting with Patricia as planned. Is that all right with you, Jess?''

She had to harness her laughter. Derek's face fell like a cement block. Obviously he'd started to ask Holmes to pick up Patricia, but his plan was foiled. Jess turned to Holmes and gave him a bright smile. ''Certainly, Mr. Holmes, and I'm sure Derek doesn't mind.''

''Now, now. If I'm to be your escort, I insist you call me Gerald.''

''Gerald it is,'' she said, sending a syrupy grin toward Derek. ''Thank you.''

While Derek gaped, Holmes suggested a time for picking her up, and before Derek could say anything, she made an excuse to leave. For Holmes's benefit, she gave Derek a quick peck on the cheek and hurried through the door, wishing she could look back over her shoulder to see his expression.

Derek dropped the receiver onto the cradle and blasted pent-up air from his lungs. Frustrated, he stared at the Yellow Pages on his desk, wondering what to do now. He'd guaranteed he would have no trouble providing a caterer for Patricia's Monday-night cocktail party for the New Yorkers, and now he faced another catastrophe. The caterer had an emergency and couldn't fulfill the contract.

Resentment rustled up his back as he realized that things like this—unimportant in the scheme of things—took time away from his real job, which was writing stories about people in peril or follow-ups about people's survival. Exciting stuff. Just thinking about it sent an adrenaline rush through his veins.

A hand clamped Derek's shoulder and he jumped. His boss gave him a curious look.

"Sorry," Holmes said. "Didn't mean to startle you."

Rising, Derek dug out his TV smile and aimed it at him. "No problem. I was deep in thought."

"Nothing wrong, I hope."

Clearing his throat, Derek grappled with telling the truth or bald-face lying. "Nothing I can't handle. Our caterer for Monday pooped out."

Holmes took a step back before responding. "Now that is a problem. Making a good first impression is vital to our negotiations." His eyes narrowed as he searched Derek's face.

"Right, sir, I know."

Holmes then eyed the telephone book spread open on Derek's desk. "I see you're making calls."

"I've made some calls but—"

"I don't want to hear 'buts,' Derek."

"I know, sir, but I've called every caterer in town and out of town, and no one is able or willing to take on a small job like this at such short notice."

"Don't tell me that. We can't offer these men chips

and dip. What about Jess? Didn't she say she has a catering business?"

Inwardly wincing, Derek plastered a confident look on his face. In his panic, he'd already thought of Jess, but how could he ask her to bail him out of this problem?

"Jess's shop is in Cincinnati. I don't think she'd—"

"Stop thinking, Derek. Ask. If you can't find a local caterer, tell her we'll double her rates. Anyway, if the woman loves you, and I'm sure she does, she'll be happy to help us out."

Holmes's determination pressed Derek into frustration. "Don't I always take care of things, sir? I'll have a caterer hired before Monday." *If the woman loves you and I'm sure she does.* That was the problem. Where Jess was concerned, Derek lived on a slippery slope. He'd watched her gleeful expression the day before when Holmes asked if he might escort her to dinner.

Holmes clamped his hand on Derek's shoulder for the second time and gave it a squeeze. "Good," he said as he marched out of the office.

Derek stared after him, praying for a solution. He'd already called every number in the telephone book and had no idea where to turn—except Jess.

And he could already hear her response. He'd disappointed Jess so many times, canceling their dinner date, letting Holmes escort her on Friday and acting like a... He let the descriptive word drop.

Why hadn't he explained himself to Holmes yes-

terday? He'd planned to ask *him* to drive Patricia to
dinner. Instead, Holmes twisted it around and agreed
to take Jess. Why had he let things get into such a
mess?

Yet somehow, Jess always seemed to understand.

At least tonight he'd invited her to go with him to
Hart Plaza on the Detroit River for a jazz concert, and
she'd agreed. He'd looked forward to the evening all
day, and tonight he planned to show Jess a good time.
More than a good time. A memorable time.

Since their attic rendezvous, Jess couldn't get Derek out of her mind. Despite her wavering concerns,
she'd agreed to go to the jazz concert. The thought
of being alone with him sent her emotions in every
direction—wanting him, yet knowing it was too
strange…too soon. Knowing it impossible. Two people meeting again after all these years both struggling
with career shifts didn't have time for a relationship.
And Jess didn't intend to be a one-night stand. But
an evening of jazz along the river sounded fun. And
safe.

When the time came to leave, Jess slid into Derek's
car dressed in black slacks and a warm red sweater
in case the evening was cool.

Looking at Derek in the sport coat and slacks that
he'd worn to the studio, Jess wondered if she was
dressed appropriately. "Will I be warm enough?" she
asked, hoping he'd suggest a different outfit if she'd
dressed too casually.

"I'll keep you warm," he said. "You look great."

She accepted his compliment, thinking that he looked better than great.

Traffic was moving and in a short time they reached downtown Detroit. When they left the underground parking lot, Jess steered Derek toward the river's edge.

She'd played a rotten trick on him yesterday when Holmes had misunderstood Derek's request. Maybe it had worked out for the best. The situation would put Derek in his place for once, after all the years he'd tormented her. That thought survived her past attitudes. She pushed it away. In her heart she'd have loved to go with Derek.

As they walked hand in hand along the bank of the Detroit River, Jess looked across the water at the Windsor skyline. Derek talked about his busy schedule and stressful day. Though he hadn't said anything, she sensed he was avoiding telling her something important. Not wanting to burden the evening with problems, she didn't press.

The sun lowered in the sky, and people wandered toward the outdoor amphitheater. They followed, and sitting on the stone bench, Jess watched the evening breeze rustle Derek's bronze hair. When the music began, she grinned as his foot kept rhythm. Finally he looked relaxed and content. For once, she felt relaxed, too.

Yet she still wondered if something had been on his mind earlier as they talked. She searched his face, but his eyes were shrouded in shadow and his thoughts were hidden.

After the concert, they crossed the street to a hotel lounge, where Derek ordered wine. He slid his hand across the table and rested it on hers.

"Great concert," Derek said. "I haven't been to a concert here in a long time."

"It's been eons for me, too," Jess said. "And such a beautiful evening. The skyline, the city lights reflected in the river, the music. Thanks for a special evening."

He drew nearer and cupped her hand between both of his. "Jess, I hope you understand what happened yesterday. I'd hoped that—"

"I understand. I saw what happened. You'll make the best of it."

"We will," he said, searching her face. "In another week you'll be going back to Cincinnati. I don't want that, Jess."

"We don't always get what we want," she said, afraid to hear what he had to say.

He wrapped his hand more tightly around hers. "I don't know, Jess. I've changed since you've come back into my life…and I'm glad."

"It's my life that I've come back to, Derek. Our lives are up in the air. We're both in the middle of changes. I'm uncertain about so many things."

"Don't be uncertain." He lifted her hand to his lips, and his breath brushed her fingers, sending a tingle down her arm. "I care about you. I think you know that."

Jess's pulse accelerated. "I care about you, too, but…I'm confused. Things are moving too fast. For years my memories of you could have lined a litter box. Now…now I'm like a pendulum, swinging back and forth and not certain which side is reality.''

"Don't fight it, Jess. Remember the afternoon in the attic? You can't deny what happened there between us. We both felt it. Passion, but more than that. Connection. I'm not good at poetry. I write news. But what happened up there was great news to me.''

"Forget the attic. We had dust fairies in our eyes. Attics are nostalgic and dreamy. The world is reality. And our worlds are very separate. Our lives are unstable. We both have changing career plans. You're looking for a promotion. A position that will take time and concentration, and I'm planning to sever my partnership and struggle on my own.'' *And come home.* The thought shuffled through her like a cozy Christmas.

Jess lifted the stemmed glass and sipped the pale-amber wine.

Though Derek's face showed a twinge of dismay, he rallied in a pulse beat. "I hear the words, but face it, we create our own reality. Who cares what happened years ago? We're new people today with a new friendship. More than a friendship, Jess. Think about it. Chew on it awhile like one of your little 'doovers.' Give this a chance.''

His silly comment brought a smile to her lips. "I'll keep quiet—for now. Depressed isn't where I want to be tonight. If I didn't care about you, I'd have no problem. Let's enjoy the moment.''

His spirit brightened, and a tender smile washed

over his face. "You're wonderful, Jess. Talented, successful, lovable." He raised his hand to her cheek and brushed a finger down it.

Jess pressed a palm to her chest to still the hummingbirds there. What should she do? Forget her fears? Forget reality?

His gaze searched hers, his eyes beseeching. "You've been my fantasy for years, Jess. You've stepped into my life. You've given it balance and pleasure. And here I am pleading again."

He clasped her shoulders and in his eyes, she saw longing. "I need you, Jess. I don't know what I'll do without you."

Unsettled yearning raced through Jess. She'd mouthed words, but she knew that Derek had captured her heart as no one had before. She studied his serious face. His eyes, his lips, the shy smile. How could she turn him down?

She felt herself weaken. He wanted her and she wanted him. Seeing his longing, her fortitude vanished. With her armor falling to her feet, Jess put her hand over his.

"How much, Derek? Tell me how badly you need me."

Chapter Eight

Astounded at Jess's response, Derek stared at her, speechless. She leaned across the table, her eyes glazed with emotion. The sounds of the restaurant faded like the distant hum of bees, and all Derek could hear was her voice and the beating of his heart. Her giving spirit wrapped around him like a summer breeze.

"Are you sure, Jess? I don't want to ask anything that you'll regret, but I'm desperate."

Her expression wavered until she riveted her warm, tender gaze to his. "I'm willing, Derek...if you're sure. Just ask me."

Relief flooded him. Yet he hesitated. Her face glowed with compassion, and he hated to have the feeling fade when he detailed his request. Still she looked so sure he had to trust her. "Thank you for understanding, Jess. I'll never forget this."

"I won't either, Derek."

The air sparked with expectation. "I know this is your vacation, so your offer is doubly generous."

As he spoke, an odd look inched across her face, but he charged ahead. "The caterer I hired for Monday's small cocktail party canceled, and I'll be in hot water up to my... I guess you don't need the graphic details, but I need your help so badly I..."

He paused, seeing Jess's face waver between confusion and anger. What had he done?

The scene dashed through Derek's mind.

His stupidity washed over him like a broken water main. His pea-size brain had segued from romance and relationship to his predicament with hardly a pause for breath.

"Jess, I'm sorry. You thought—"

"I thought nothing." Her voice snapped with fire, and her cheeks burned with the same red heat. "What do you need?"

He opened his mouth to explain, but she barreled ahead.

"Obviously you need a caterer. Sure, why not? I'm leaving in a week, but why should I endanger your promotion by leaving you in the lurch with your boss?"

"Please...understand that—"

"What is there to understand?"

Derek's chest tightened, seeing the mortification he'd caused. If he could erase what happened, he'd do it. Losing his promotion was nothing compared to hurting Jess.

"I'll help you on one condition," she fumed. "We work side by side on this project. I don't have assistants here, and I'm not doing a project like this one alone. You arrange the time to help me, and I'll—"

"No, Jess. Forget it." Her dig held a half-truth. "I'm sorry I asked. I was stupid to even bring up the idea."

"I insist. I'll have Louise fax some recipes. Tell me how many guests, and I'll make you a star."

"Come on, Jess. Let's get out of here." He signaled the waiter for their bill, then tossed the money and tip on the table.

Jess's arm stiffened as he guided her through the lounge and out into the cool evening air. His mind riddled with thought, he nearly dragged her through the parking lot until, in the darkness, he stopped and turned her to face him.

"Look at me." He tilted her face to his, and in the dusky light, moisture glistened on her lashes. "I'm a fool, Jess. My thoughts were so focused on my job I didn't realize what my words sounded like."

He put his arm around her and felt her rigid stance as he drew her against him. "Can't you see I feel the same as you? I need you, not for making little sandwiches, but for being so wonderful. I'm sorry I'm so dense."

She looked at him, frustration written on her face. "I can't believe I was about to crawl into the sack with you. And for what? Nothing, because all you wanted was a tray of hors d'oeuvres. I'm ashamed of myself."

"Jess, no one has ever meant as much to me as you. I promise you. No one. I wasn't thinking."

He rested his cheek against her hair, stirred by the exotic fragrance. "Jess, you mean more to me than a fling. I'm not asking you to crawl into the sack or anywhere. When I make love with you, it'll be slow and wonderful on a bed of roses. Minus the thorns." He searched her face for a smile, even a tiny one.

Her face remained stoic.

Frustrated, Derek opened the car door, and Jess climbed inside. He didn't know what he'd do about the caterer, but he wouldn't allow her to fix him a glass of water and an aspirin—which he needed desperately—let alone hors d'oeuvres for a cocktail party.

They rode in silence except for the inward sound of him kicking himself. When they pulled into the garage, she swung open her door.

Before she escaped, he captured her arm. "Give me a punch, Jess. I deserve it. I can't bear to see you hurt."

He looked at her, his eyes begging for one word, one small sign that she believed him. "I know you don't think I'm being truthful, but I've been crazy about you since high school. I always wondered why I never got even close to a proposal with another woman. I tried to imagine myself married, but every woman I dated lacked something I couldn't put my finger on." He rested his palm against her cheek. "That something was you. I deserve a slap for my thoughtlessness."

Like the crack of a whip, her hand sailed through the air and whacked him on the side of the face. Stunned, he stared at her. He'd made the suggestion, but he'd meant it figuratively. The harsh reality stung his cheek and his pride.

Jess looked as shocked as he felt. She covered her face, and his heart melted. He wrapped her in his arms. He'd insulted her, offended her to the quick. He ached to kiss the tears from her eyes.

Drawing her hands from her face, Derek tilted her chin upward and faltered.

Instead of tears, he was greeted with a burst of laughter.

He felt his jaw droop like a wilting tulip until he clamped his mouth closed.

"I'm sorry, Derek. I can't believe I hit you that hard. Not that you don't deserve it."

He rubbed his cheek. "You do have quite a punch. I'll remember not to suggest that again."

The ridiculous situation made him grin, and he brushed his finger along her laugh lines and across her lips. "You're beautiful, Jess."

"You're not so bad yourself, Mr. Television. But you humiliated me tonight." Her expression relaxed and her face brightened. "I suppose this sacrifice should totally convince your boss that we're serious about each other."

"It will," Derek said. "I promise...and I promise something else. The next time you hear me say I need you, I'll mean it the way you thought I meant it."

She laid her finger across his lips. "And I don't want to hear you say it for a long time. I mean it."

"Promise," he said, crossing his heart. "Though my lips are silent, my heart is speaking."

She shook her head. "And you tell me you're not poetic."

Friday evening Gerald Holmes arrived at seven o'clock and graciously escorted Jess to his luxury sedan. At the restaurant, Duff's on the Lake, Jess paused beside him as the maître d' prepared their table. She waited as her eyes adjusted to the dimmed lighting before scanning the crowd.

With menus tucked beneath his tuxedoed arm, the headwaiter led them to a cozy table along the broad windows looking out on Lake St. Clair. With a flourish he handed them each an elegant menu. As Jess perused it, she furtively eyed the doorway, waiting for Derek and Patricia.

"You look lovely this evening, Jess," Holmes said.

"Thank you, Mr.—Gerald." She looked down at the unique vintage dress out of the forties she'd bought at Patti Smith's Collectibles. "It's an old dress." She grinned at her ambiguity.

"It's charming." He lowered his eyes and slid the menu onto the table. "I'm sorry my daughter dragged Derek away from you, but...the pleasure is mine. I would have come alone, I'm afraid."

"Derek said you're widowed."

"Nearly three years." He lifted his hand and turned the delicate bouquet at the table's center. "I'm a family man, Jess, and I suppose that's why I've spoiled my daughter.''

"You love her. There's nothing wrong with that."

His face brightened. "I hope you're right." He sent her a sad smile and turned toward the doorway. "Here they are."

Jess's attention shot toward the maître d's station. Patricia clung to Derek's arm like a drowning swimmer, but Jess's heart lifted when she saw his eyes meet her own.

"Sorry we're late," Derek said. "We ran into a few snags."

He helped Patricia to her seat, then hurried to kiss Jess's cheek. She gave him a sweet smile, watching Patricia squirm.

The meal progressed with talk of the upcoming visit. She listened with half an ear, enjoying the feel of Derek's foot against hers beneath the table.

As they finished their main course, a three-piece band made its way to the small platform, and soon easy-listening music drifted softly through the air— old tunes, classical standards about the same vintage as her dress. Holmes rose and extended his hand to Jess. "Would you dance with your appreciative escort? What other old man will have such a beautiful woman on his arm?"

"You're not old, Gerald, and I'd love to," she said, and followed him onto the floor, touched by his gentleness.

Moving to the slow song, Jess looked over at Patricia, whose glamorous face had turned prunelike with her father's words. While she leaned across the table, buzzing in Derek's ear, Derek's eyes focused on Jess.

When the love song ended, a Latin rhythm caught her off guard. Holmes chuckled. "I haven't danced the samba in years. Want to give it a try?"

Though afraid she'd make a fool of herself, Jess agreed, and they moved to the exotic beat. She had to give the man credit. He knew how to dance and made it easy for her to follow the slow rhythmic steps. Suddenly he drew her close with a twirl and a deep backward dip. Unconsciously, she closed her eyes momentarily, and when she opened them again, in her upside-down world, she saw Derek's surprised face.

"My word!" Derek shot upward with the momentum of a lunar rocket.

Holmes lifted her with whiplash speed as she grabbed the top of her dress, sensing that gravity may have exposed more than her presence.

"I think I got a bit carried away," Holmes said when they returned to their seats. His face was ruddy and his eyes sparkled. "Did I frighten you?" he asked Derek.

"Only surprised me, sir."

"That makes two of us," Patricia muttered. "Remember your age, Father."

Jess slid into her chair and looked at Patricia. "Your father is young at heart. I wouldn't worry about him."

Patricia's face paled, and Jess sensed that for once the woman was at a loss for words.

They sat in silence until a slow tune began again. "I haven't danced in years," Holmes said. "You don't mind, Derek, if I dance with Jess again?" He rose and Jess joined him on the dance floor.

Speechless, Derek gaped at her gliding across the floor with his boss. Why had Jess accepted Holmes's dinner invitation? She was supposed to be *his* woman. That was their pretense.

He sipped wine and watched her. Foolish question. He'd disappointed her again. She'd done him a great service leading Holmes to believe that they were serious about each other. Jess had been thinking of him and his chance for promotion. What had he done for her? Nothing. Not even escorted her to this dinner.

Watching her dance, Derek admired Jess's dress. So often Jess covered herself with loose-fitting sweaters that hid her lovely figure. The royal-blue one she wore now wrapped around her shoulders and dipped in a V, exposing the creamy rise of her breasts. The silky cloth clung to her shapely hips, and he followed its journey to her well-formed calves.

"I'm not interrupting you, am I?" Patricia growled. "You seem to be miles away."

He flinched, realizing his thoughtlessness. "I'm thinking about the work I have facing me tomorrow." But he found himself focused on Jess again—her deep-brown hair, like chocolate, loosened and spread over her velvety pale shoulders. "I should call it an evening."

"What?" Patricia lowered her voice. "You've changed, Derek."

"I hope for the better."

"That depends. Better for whom? I thought you enjoyed working for Daddy," she murmured in his ear.

"I enjoy my job, Patricia. You know I do." He struggled to keep his rising tone below the sound of the music and a smile plastered on his face. "Look I asked Jess to help with the catering on Monday. I won't let down the station or your father."

"I'm sure the evening will be delightful," Patricia said.

She looked away, and Derek's stomach churned at the mess he'd created. He'd had about as much as he could take of Patricia's threats. At this point, the job didn't mean much to him anymore. To his relief the music ended, and Holmes and Jess returned to the table.

Derek fought his desire to ask Jess to dance...to hold her against him on the dance floor. The evening had already created untold stress that he'd have to live with for the next few days as they entertained their New York guests. Winning the battle over his desire, he used common sense.

"I'm afraid I have to leave," Derek said. "As I explained to Patricia, I have a busy day tomorrow. We want everything to be perfect Monday evening." He rose, then as if having an afterthought, turned to Holmes. "Do you mind driving Patricia home?"

"Not at all," he said.

Derek extended his hand to Holmes and nodded to Patricia. "I'll see both of you tomorrow."

To Derek's surprise, Jess rose from the table. "Would you mind if I join you, Derek, since we're going to the same place? It'll save Gerald a trip."

"Not at all if—"

"No problem," Holmes said. "Makes perfect sense to me."

Patricia remained silent.

"Thank you, Gerald, for the lovely evening." She leaned down and kissed his cheek. "I have a little suggestion for you."

He grinned at her. "Suggestion?"

Jess nodded. "When you get home tonight, look in a mirror. You're a handsome man—and a very good dancer. You ought to share that charm with some lonely lady. Life is too short to spend it alone."

His eyes softened, and he clutched her shoulders and planted a kiss on her cheek. "Derek's a lucky man. You're a delightful young woman."

She smiled and turned toward Derek. He steered her toward the door, surprised and touched by her thoughtful words to Holmes.

Outside, she paused, her face colored by emotion. "Was I wrong, Derek? He's a lonely man who dotes on his daughter and overlooks his own needs. I like him. I really do."

"I'm proud of you, Jess. What you said was kind."

"And truthful," she added.

Eyeing her spike heels, Derek clasped her arm and assisted her over the rough pavement to the car. He fumbled for his key while his thoughts focused on Jess, washed in silver moonlight. Her vivid blue dress shimmered in the soft glow, contrasting the milky white of her skin.

"Jess."

She tilted her head, waiting.

"I look at you, then at a woman like Patricia and…" He touched her cheek. "I shouldn't say your names in the same breath. You're an amazing woman."

With her face lifted to his, he regarded her lips— gently parted and enticing.

"Why are you looking at me like that?" she asked.

He didn't answer. Instead, he drew her into his arms, and kissed those lips, quieting her, but not quieting his pounding heart. The thud hammered in his chest like restless warriors.

And like a warrior, he wanted to have her, slip the silken dress from her body and cover her in pink silk and lace.

His eager mouth pressed hers until he eased back, moving his mouth more softly, more gently against her parted lips.

With abandon, Jess threw her arms around his neck and moved with him, her lips firm yet soft beneath his, her body yielding.

Lifting her off her feet, Derek swung her into his arms.

Jess let out a cry, but he silenced her again with his mouth. When his eyes opened, he stood in the dimly lit parking lot like Rhett Butler with Scarlett in his arms.

He carried her to his car, opened the passenger door

and lowered Jess to the seat. When he climbed in the driver side, he clasped her hand and kissed her fingers. A sound surfaced from deep in his throat.

Where would they go from here?

Chapter Nine

Jess opened her eyes and peered at the narrow ridge of sun peeking beneath the window shade. She'd apparently slept late. Sleep hadn't come easy as she had struggled with the barrage of emotions vaulting through her. She could no longer forget them or push them back into a corner of her mind. They'd grown in size and shape and had filled her with questions and concerns.

Even if she was confident about Derek's feelings for her, their lives were separated by complex careers and pasts too riddled with familiarity. He was Meg's kid brother.

Before she'd arrived in Royal Oak, Jess had given thought to buying Louise's share of the catering business, but not leaving the area or developing a whole new clientele. She'd spent years nurturing the present business. In Cincinnati she had a multitude of good contacts. But in Michigan she would have to start over again.

And Derek? His future seemed up in the air. The anchor position. And he'd casually mentioned New York...or was the Big Apple only a dream? Whatever he chose, she wouldn't want less for him.

Since coming home to Michigan, Jess had seen things change so quickly in their relationship. But would the changes last? And could she trust what she felt in her heart and witnessed in Derek's eyes? Summer flings. Shipboard romances. Could her feelings be only for the here and now, and not for a lifetime?

On top of that, could she believe in Derek? With his handsome smile and charisma, he could charm her into anything. The memory of the evening before shivered through her. Would she be only another conquest—his sister's skinny friend whom he'd taunted and jeered at through high school? Winning her over might be his idea of a good laugh.

If so, the laugh would be on Derek. She pulled her dented and rusted armor—as wavering as it was—into her consciousness. Somehow she'd come out the winner.

Jess rolled over and lifted her head. Though it was Saturday, Derek had mentioned he'd be at the studio in the morning. While he worked, she had to prepare for the shindig she'd agreed to cater.

She swung her feet to the floor and collected her thoughts. First she had to call Louise and ask her to fax the recipes—ones she could handle on short notice and without special equipment. Then she needed to make a shopping list.

Jess dressed, and headed downstairs, she read Meg's note—Meg was running errands. After a quick breakfast, Jess made the call, waited and pulled the recipes from Derek's fax machine as they came through. She spent a few minutes studying the ingredients, then the shopping list rolled from her pencil: chèvre and fresh Parmesan cheese, eggs, whipping cream, large white mushrooms, Belgian endive, shrimp. She hoped a simple variety of canapés would suffice.

When Derek arrived home, she turned him around and pushed him back out the door. "You got me into this, so you can suffer right along with me."

He gave her a pathetic grin, but she slapped the grocery list into his hand, anyway. "Together, remember?"

Jess decided to rub it in good. "And maybe we'll run into your boss at the market. Wouldn't he be impressed?"

"I suppose, but…"

She arched an eyebrow. "But what? You don't want me to leave you without a nibble to your name, do you? Do you want your New York guests chowing on crackers and cheese spread?"

"By help, I meant I'd show you where to find my pans." He eyed her a moment, then grinned. "Apparently you meant something different. You expect me to make those dainty, little, bite-size things."

"You got it," Jess said, then paused. "You didn't forget to call the rental place, did you?"

"No, everything ordered. Crystal, linen, the lot."

"That's what I want to hear." She gave him a gentle nudge and climbed into his car.

The shopping trip proved trying, since Derek was little help. He didn't seem to know a kipper from a caper. With her own perseverance, Jess finally stood in the checkout line, her basket filled with chèvre, black olives, caviar and all the other makings of the party fare.

Back home, Jess tensed when she looked at the kitchen clock. Tonight was the centennial reception. "I need time to dress," she said, propping the sacks on the counter.

"I'll put the stuff away while you get ready," Derek said. "I'm already pretty—without makeup."

"You're pretty questionable." She sent him a grin, but accepted his offer graciously and hurried to her room.

In less than an hour Derek had parked in the high-school lot. Jess stepped from the car, but when he reached her side, reality smacked her. She'd not thought about walking into the reception with her friend's pesky kid brother on her arm.

Anxiety raced up her spine as she walked into the crowded entrance of the school assembly hall. A blur of faces floated past, some distantly familiar, others totally unknown.

Music drifted from the open double doors, and Derek steered her inside where a deejay slapped CDs into his player while couples drifted onto the large wooden floor to dance to the latest tunes.

Soft drinks and snacks had been spread out on long tables, and Derek poured two drinks into paper cups, and handed her one.

While Jess sipped the soda, occasional squeals echoed across the crammed room as people recognized old friends and classmates. While a TV fan cornered Derek, Jess worked her way through the throng, greeting old acquaintances and sharing the latest news.

The lights dimmed. Derek found her in the crowd and drew her onto the dance floor and into his arms. No one had made a negative comment about them being together, and she relaxed. Looking into Derek's confident eyes, Jess felt a sense of well-being, and she reveled in his tender embrace.

The same fresh, woodsy smell she'd enjoyed the day he'd rescued her on the freeway returned the image of how he'd looked then. She could see his strong arms working the jack while his wet shirt clung to his broad chest. She pictured the tight jeans outlining his powerful legs. The image made her shiver.

"Something wrong?" he asked in her ear. His hand against her lower back drew her closer.

His excitement greeted her at the nearness, and she blushed. "No. Everything's right," she murmured.

Her arms tightened around him, and against her plans, she yielded to his eager touch, yearning for more and wondering why she tormented herself.

Derek gazed at her, his eyes heavy and misted with emotion. He whispered her name and his lips nuzzled her earlobe before brushing across her cheek. Caution rifled through her as she ignited at his touch.

When a hand clasped his shoulder, Derek flinched, and with a final rhythmic sway, he paused. Jess lifted her eyes to a man she didn't recognize.

"Bill Greene," Derek said in greeting. His arm still around her waist, Derek released Jess's hand and clasped the man's shoulder.

The name darted through Jess's memory, then skidded to a halt. Bill Greene had been one of Derek's football buddies. She cringed and longed to sink into the flooring.

Bill's attention turned to Jess, and a glimmer of recognition slithered across his face. "This couldn't be..." His gaze traveled her length, lingering on her breasts and hips, then returned toward her face. "Not Frenchie," he said, a leer tugging his mouth. "Frenchie and Big Derek. Unbelievable."

"Cool it," Derek said. "We're adults now, Bill. I presume you remember Jess?" He turned his tense face toward her. "Bill and I played ball together."

"I remember," Jess said.

Bill caught Jess's free hand. "My turn, Derek. You don't mind, do you?" He wrapped his arm around her and tugged her toward him.

"Are you okay with this?" Derek asked her, his expression grim.

Though she wanted to cling to Derek, she nodded and allowed Bill to lead her into the music's sway.

"Couldn't help myself," Bill said. "You've certainly grown into a beautiful woman, Jess."

She held herself erect to avoid contact. "Thank you."

"And quite the cradle robber, too."

Her body went rigid.

"Relax," he said, grinning.

After a few turns, the song ended, and catching him off guard, Jess stepped from his grasp. "Sorry, Bill. I need to make a trip to the ladies' room."

He looked disappointed. "Later, then."

As she hurried away, a new voice called her name from the crush of bodies.

Jess turned and saw a plump woman, vaguely familiar, hurrying toward her.

The woman grasped her shoulders. "Lorraine Kaminski. It's the same old me, just a little bigger."

Jess smiled warmly. "Lorraine. How in the world have you been?"

"Great, Jess…and I see you're doing oddly well."

Her comment halted Jess's pleasant memories. "Oddly well?"

Lorraine used her shoulder to gesture across the room.

Toward Derek.

Jess's spirits sagged, and she struggled to plaster an amiable grin on her face. "Ah, now I understand."

"You do…but I don't. What are you doing with Derek Randolph? He's the last person in the world I would have expected to see with you." She turned and looked about the room. "Where's Meg?"

Jess shook her head. "Coming later, I think." An unpleasant sensation seeped through her. She and

Derek. Unbelievable. Odd. What else could she expect? Would this be people's reaction forever?

"I can't really blame you," Lorraine said, her face suddenly etched with remorse for her blunder. "He's so good-looking...and so popular."

Jess paid little attention to their conversation now, and as soon as possible made an excuse to escape her old friend.

As she hurried off, Derek caught her hand. "What's the matter?"

She pulled away. "No matter how much we try to forget the past, people won't let us."

"Bill's one person, Jess."

"It's not only Bill. I just got more from my old friend, Lorraine." The situation hung in her mind. "Give them time, Derek. We'll have them rolling in the aisles."

He wove his fingers through hers and steered her back through the double doors. "Let's get some air."

The cool night air fluttered across Jess's arms, and Derek drew her to his side, his warm hands caressing her icy skin. Alone in the darkness, he lifted his hand to her chin and tilted her face to his. "What can I say, Jess? Can't we just laugh it off and ignore it?"

"It's not that easy. You know that."

"What's more important? People's idiotic comments...or us. Our friendship. You know how I feel about you."

"Maybe I'm overreacting, but—"

Before she finished, his lips found hers, and she yielded without contemplation. He caressed her arms and shoulders until his hand reached her back, molding her against him. A sigh slid from her aching throat.

Why did everything seem all right when she was in Derek's arms? Though he was part of the problem, when she was with him, she felt safe and protected. Her heartstrings had tangled with his. Yet she wondered if she could ever allow herself to unsnarl her feelings and enjoy the relationship.

Sunday, as Derek promised, he stood beside Jess in the kitchen, elbow-deep in canapé recipes. They'd made no reference to the previous evening. The smug looks of old classmates, the constant reminders of the past, had been pushed aside for the moment.

Jess had promised to help Derek's cause, and she tried to give it her full attention. As she worked on the canapés, her mind stirred with questions. Why did she allow other people's comments to bother her? Derek had proved himself. Or had he?

Since she'd arrived, he'd made promises he'd later broken, taunted her with the old nicknames, let another woman occupy his time. Yet…he'd been tender and apologetic. Why couldn't she trust him?

Working together in the kitchen, she tried to concentrate, but each time their arms brushed or their hands reached for the same item, her pulse went up another notch. She was behaving like a child told not to eat the cookies. Around Derek, she couldn't wait to get her hands into the cookie jar.

The aroma of baked cheese, eggs and scallions tingled Jess's taste buds, and she crossed to the oven to pull out the miniature chèvre tarts.

"How about a taste test?" Derek asked, sidling behind her.

She lifted one from the baking sheet and blew on it. "It's too hot," she said.

"I can handle it," he whispered, his warm breath brushing her ear. He turned her around and flashed a mischievous grin.

Jess lifted the tart toward him, and like a baby bird, he opened his mouth while she slipped the morsel between his lips. He captured her fingers along with the tart and kissed them.

Wrapped in pleasure, she watched him savor the tart, and when his tongue darted out to clean away the last crumb, she pulled away in an effort to control her reaction. "Good?" she asked.

"Delicious. And so are you."

She ignored his playful comment and steered him back to his task at the counter while she mixed a delicate cheesy batter. When she finished, Derek spooned it in circles on the baking sheets, creating melt-in-the-mouth pastry puffs. He'd followed her directions without a squawk. She demonstrated a technique, and he duplicated it. He'd stuck to their bargain. Sometimes he amazed her.

When they finished, he leaned against the counter and folded his arms. "Finally. Done."

"Don't fold those arms too tight. We still have cleanup," Jess said. His blue eyes played havoc with her heartbeat.

"We've been at this cooking stuff for hours. Come here for a minute." He spread his arms toward her.

She held her ground, nudged by a thought. "Did you tell Holmes I'm catering the cocktail party?"

Derek tucked his hands in his pockets and jiggled his keys. "He knows. He suggested we hire you."

"He did?" Disappointment struck her like a rock. She'd agreed to do this for Derek, not his boss.

"He couldn't resist your charm." He sidled toward her, dreamy-eyed.

She backed away. "I'll tell you one thing. The next time you need a favor, don't look my way."

His smile faded, and Derek came to a stop. "I thought about asking you before Holmes suggested it, Jess, but I didn't want to take advantage. I..." He paused, his eyes filled with apology.

She shrugged. "You have taken advantage, but it makes no difference. I agreed to help you, anyway."

"I know. That's why I lo...think you're wonderful."

His faltering words took her by surprise. Had he almost said love? Her irritation softened, and she stood in silence looking at him—so strong, yet so vulnerable.

"Let's get this cleaned up. It's late," she said, and began rinsing the bowls and measuring cups and dropping them into the dishwasher.

He rinsed the dishcloth and wiped down the counter, then stopped. "Hungry? I'm starving."

"I'm almost too tired."

"Look," he said, finally capturing her arm. "Let's

order a pizza, or better yet, let's go to the Pizza Stop down the street.'' He slid his arm around her waist and drew her so close she could feel the ripple of muscles in his chest. ''What do you say?''

Looking into his eyes, she couldn't say a thing. Her heart rested in her throat while her chest filled with butterflies. She nodded, and he kissed the end of her nose.

''Let's go,'' he said, pulling out his car keys.

She washed her hands and flung the towel over the back of a chair before following him as if he were the Pied Piper.

Not ten minutes later they were seated at a small table eyeing the menu.

''No anchovies,'' Jess said, ''but anything else is fine.''

He placed the order and took a swig from the largest beer mug she'd ever seen.

She leaned back, enjoying the moment, feeling comfortable and relaxed for the first time in days. ''This is nice. Nothing fancy. No pretension. Just pizza, beer and you.'' The tempting aromas stirred her appetite. Her belly rumbled and, embarrassed, she covered it with her hand.

Derek chuckled.

''I can't seem to quiet the alien,'' she said.

''I knew you had some deep dark secret.''

When she put her hand on the table, he caught it in his. ''We should move away from here—someplace where no one knows our past. No past. No problems. Only the future.''

The warm thought eased over her until her plans shuffled into her mind—bringing her business home where everyone knew her. She lifted her gaze to Derek's and nodded. "A nice fantasy."

Looking past her, Derek's face morphed from a smile to panic.

A voice boomed in Jess's ear. "Big Der-reeck! Number thirty-three comin' out on the field."

Jess look up as a huge, burly stranger wrestled Derek from his seat with a loud grunt. His chanting left no question in Jess's mind as to his and Derek's relationship.

He pushed Derek back to his seat and plopped down on the booth bench beside him. "So how are you, man?"

"Hey, Plowboy," Derek said, less than enthusiastic and giving him a high five. "How've you been?"

"Good. You back for the centennial, too?" he asked.

"No, I live here. I bought the old house from Meg after my mom died."

"Sorry about your mom. How's Meg?" He pulled his attention away from Derek, and his eyes lit on Jess as if he expected her to be Meg.

Jess stared at the man, trying to put a name to the face.

"Don't think we've met," he said.

"This is Jess," Derek said. "She was Meg's friend. Graduated before we did." He turned toward Jess with a subtle rolling of his eyes. "Jess, you remember Pete Plowver, don't you? We called him 'Red' in high school.''

Sadly, Jess remembered. "Red Plowver. Sure."

"Jess?" Pete leaned forward. "You'd think I'd remember a babe like you."

"I'm Jessamy Cosette," she said.

When he heard her full name, recognition shot across his face. "Not Frenchie!" His gaze slid over her. "You're Derek's old 'String Bean.'"

He shot Derek a look while a crooked smile slithered across his face. He aimed the smirk at Jess. "Who'd have thought? You're a fox." He gave Derek a poke in the ribs. "Time sure can work wonders."

"Sometimes," Jess said, wishing it had worked on Pete.

"Can't believe the two of you are sitting at the same table." He shifted his gaze from Derek to Jess and back, then let out a guffaw that captured the attention of most everyone nearby.

Jess cringed, wishing she could sink through the floor.

Pete kept his tennis-volley gaze going until the waitress placed the pizza on the table and his attention turned to food. He snagged the waitress, and while he ordered, Derek sent Jess a look of apology.

Her stomach churned as she realized Pete wasn't leaving.

Periodically the bruiser snatched a piece of pepperoni from their pizza. Between snatches Pete licked his fingers, then wiped his mouth on the back of his hand. Jess stared at her dinner and had second thoughts about having another piece.

When they escaped the restaurant, Derek didn't make any comment until they were settled in the car. "I'm sorry he ruined our evening. Please tell me I was never that obnoxious."

Jess sat in silence.

"Come on. I wasn't. I couldn't have been." He eyed her again, but she only gazed at him without a sound.

"No wonder you hated me, Jess."

Though she ached with the reality, Derek's pleading eyes triggered her response. "That was the past, remember? No past…only the future."

"Some genius said that once. Am I right?" He leaned across the seat and pressed his lips to her cheek.

Although she smiled, she wondered if even a genius could bury their past and offer them a future.

Chapter Ten

Derek wasn't a stupid man. Though Jess said words to the contrary, he knew she cared about him.

How did he know that? Because she'd forgiven him for his years of taunting and teasing. Because she was willing to give her vacation time to help him in a time of need. Because she kissed him and sighed and nestled in his arms like a woman in love.

Derek lay in bed weighing his future. His spot on the station had been a dream—one that could soon become a reality. And why? Because he had worked hard. Because he had talent. Because he cared about people. And he would succeed without the boss's daughter's help.

Though he considered himself a man of action—hurrying from one breaking story to another and beating down doors to bring the viewers a compelling special report—lately, with Jess in his life, he'd fallen short. But the time had come to be a man of action again. With his thoughts balancing on the scales of decision, Derek swung out of bed.

The next few days were strategic. With a successful cocktail party and smooth negotiations, Derek would feel relief. He would have run the fifty yards and made his touchdown. If his energy and hard work didn't make Holmes happy, so be it. He'd find a fresh dream.

Monday had arrived, and with his mind whirring, Derek rose, dressed and headed to work. In the late afternoon, when he heard the visitors had checked into their hotel, Derek left the television studio and stopped at the rental store. With the supplies piled in his SUV, he drove to Patricia's exclusive riverfront condo, where he'd agreed to meet Jess while Patricia visited the hair salon.

The guest list had risen to twenty-four, and Derek stared at the four large boxes filled with crystal, silver trays, linens and glassware, wondering how he would get them all into the elevator.

Grateful for help from Patricia's neighbor, he finally opened the door with a key she'd provided and wrestled the boxes into the kitchen. Within a few minutes, the bell rang, and he buzzed in Jess. Once she'd organized the supplies, Derek opened a box of linens, pulled out a large white apron and wrapped it around his suit. "I have to change my shirt and tie, but that's it, so I can help a little until the guests arrive."

Jess faltered. "Help a little? I thought we were in this together." A frown wrinkled her forehead.

Surprise shot through him. He assumed she knew he'd be busy during the party. "Jess, I'm sorry. You didn't think I could be in here all evening, did you? Holmes told me to mingle and make a good impression."

She stood as if transfixed, holding a large silver tray in her hand.

He rested his palm on her arm. "You didn't really think I could work the kitchen with you, did you?"

"I'd hoped. How am I going to do this alone?" She set the tray on the counter and kept her eyes lowered as she loaded it with the cheese pastry puffs. "Who'll keep the trays filled?"

Flushed, she peered around the room while Derek followed her gaze, aware of the containers of canapés to be arranged on trays and others she still needed to prepare.

Her face filled with panic. "I hope you have a bartender."

"He'll be here. Don't worry about that." Derek took the tray from her hand. "Tell me what I can do."

Jess let out a deep sigh. She could tell him what to do all right, but it wouldn't be what he expected.

She gestured to the shrimp. "You can put those on a tray. Cover the bottom with lettuce." She pointed to the container of washed and dried leaves. "Then put that crystal bowl in the middle of the tray and fill it with this sauce." She handed him the jar of cocktail sauce she'd made the day before.

As he turned to follow her instructions, the outer door slammed and Jess knew that Patricia had arrived. The click of stiletto heels sounded in the marble foyer, then faded to silence as she reached the carpeting. The scent of her perfume arrived before she did.

"Well, isn't this cozy," Patricia murmured, pausing in the doorway. "Julia Child and her aproned assistant." She scanned the room, eyeing the attractive trays of hors d'oeuvres. "Don't these look yummy," she said, clicking across the flooring and grabbing a small cheese puff.

Jess stared at the empty space in her neat design and pulled another canapé from a container. She slapped it on the tray.

"Not bad. Not bad at all," Patricia said, licking her fingers.

Jess gripped the silver tray in her hand. While her blood froze with irritation, the cold metal stirred her fingers to action, but she controlled the desire to whack Patricia over the head.

"It's time to get dressed," Patricia said, glancing at her watch. She headed across the room, stopped and pivoted on her heel to focus on Jess. "Speaking of dress, where's your uniform?"

"Uniform?" Jess looked down at her comfortable loafers and her plain beige dress, protected by one of the large white aprons. In Jess's opinion, she looked more than appropriate to serve the guests. She shot a direct look at the woman. "I don't wear a uniform."

"You'll certainly wear one for this party," Patricia said, striding across the room. She swung open a door, stepped inside and returned carrying a black dress with a white apron and maid's cap. "This should fit."

The silver tray slipped from Jess's fingers and clattered against the floor.

"I'll get that," Derek said. He did so and handed it to Jess, then marched across the room. Eye to eye with Patricia, Derek snatched the uniform from her hand. "Jess doesn't wear a uniform."

He crossed the floor, tossed the uniform inside the pantry and spun around to face Patricia. "Jess is doing us a tremendous favor. A uniform isn't part of the bargain."

He slammed the pantry door. "You'd better get dressed. The guests will be arriving any minute."

Patricia's mouth fell open.

Instead of surrendering, Derek faced her as if in combat. "I'll give Jess a hand until I hear the doorbell. She has a lot to do."

Patricia arched an eyebrow and flounced through the doorway.

Jess leaned against the long, elegant counter, wondering how she'd allowed herself to get into this situation. "Go ahead, Derek. I'll manage."

He ignored her. "Let's get busy." He turned again to the shrimp.

She watched him a moment, then did as he suggested.

When the doorbell rang, Jess moved quickly to set the first trays of canapés on the long table in Patricia's luxurious dining room. The bartender sent her a smile from the living room wet bar, and Jess managed a pleasant nod. But her attention gravitated to Derek, posed at the door next to Patricia, greeting guests. She yearned to dump the tray of fancy finger foods on the carpet—or better yet on Patricia's head—and make her escape.

Though Derek focused on the guests, Jess noticed the apologetic look he sent her way. She'd been foolish to think he would have time to work with her in the kitchen. He belonged at the party with the other station personnel.

Retreating to the kitchen, Jess wiped off an empty tray and began to refill it. Another batch of mushroom caps warmed in the oven, and the aroma filled the room. She pulled the appetizer from the range.

As Jess carried the baking sheet across the room, Patricia pranced into the kitchen and leaned against the counter. "The canapés are wonderful," Patricia gushed. "I wish I were more domestic." She sent Jess a honeyed smile.

"Thanks," Jess said. "I'd be glad to share a couple of my recipes."

She turned away trying to ignore Patricia and douse the smoldering irritation that licked up her spine. She focused on the tray.

"Me?" Patricia said. "No, but you certainly look like little Miss Homebody."

"It's good for one's soul and increases humility." Jess glared into Patricia's face.

"It's a shame you didn't wear the uniform. It goes so well with these little canapés you seem to have such a talent for. Sort of loses something without them, don't you think?"

"No, I don't. You just told me how wonderful they are." She sent the woman a gracious smile.

"I'd better get back before my guests wonder where I am. By the way, don't forget to clean up. The mop's in the pantry." She turned and paraded from the kitchen.

Patricia's departing comment left Jess spitting nails. One more word, and it would truly be the woman's last. Jess could easily sail out the door— that is, if Derek's promotion wasn't on the line. She turned back to her work, swallowing her irritation.

When footsteps caught her attention again, Jess turned toward the kitchen door expecting Patricia again. Instead, a gray-haired gentleman leaned against the doorjamb with a grin and a little wave. "Looking for the rest room, but since I've found you," he said, "I must compliment the chef. The food's wonderful."

"Thanks," Jess said, keeping her eyes on the tray.

When she looked over her shoulder, he'd vanished, but before she took a relieved breath, he'd returned— and this time, came right into the kitchen.

"So what does an attractive young woman do after she's finished serving these tasty morsels?" He squeezed beside her, slipped a cheese tart from the tray and popped it into his mouth.

"She cleans up this mess and goes home." She could smell the gin on his breath.

"But what if a gentleman offered her an evening of entertainment…and perhaps his room number at the Carlton?" He brought a hand to her shoulder, then slid it down her arm.

Jess pulled away, using an empty tray as a shield, but before she needed to act, Derek darted into the room.

"How are you doing, Jess?" he asked, glaring at the back of the gentleman's head. "Mr. Fletcher, I'd like you to meet a dear friend of mine, Jessamy Cosette. She's filling in here as a personal favor."

Fletcher, obviously uncomfortable, took a step back. "Nice to meet you…Miss Cosette." He turned to Derek. "I was just complimenting her canapés."

"She's an expert cook," Derek said, grabbing the man's arm.

Fletcher turned and left the scene like an accomplice after a holdup.

A sigh escaped Jess's throat. "I'm not sure I can handle much more of this. Between Patricia's digs and the likes of Mr. Fletcher, I'm about ready to…" Though she tried to halt them, tears rose in her eyes.

Derek's face softened, and he lifted a finger and caught the moisture on her lashes. "Jess, please. I feel bad enough. Come here." He opened his arms.

As frustrated as Jess felt, his arms looked safe and inviting, and she allowed him to draw her close and snuggle her head into his chest. He took the tray from her hand and led her the few steps to the pantry. Inside, he snapped on the light and pulled her into another embrace.

Jess blinked at the setting. Why were they in the pantry? She knew. To avoid prying eyes. No matter, feeling weary and frustrated, she longed for a place of comfort and she found it in Derek's arms.

His gaze traversed her face and rested on her lips. "Jess, I don't know why I let you get into this mess. I should have used good sense, but then I seem to be short on that." He tilted her face to his. "I've acted like a fool."

His mouth lowered to hers, and unable to fight her feelings, she stood on tiptoe to meet him.

With gentle strokes, he caressed her lips with his, and she reveled in the pleasurable sensation. This was where she belonged.

Without warning, the pantry door banged open. Jess looked over in alarm.

Patricia stood at the doorway. "Are you looking for anything in particular?" she asked, her anger obvious.

"Looking for some privacy, Patricia. Jess had a bad experience with one of the guests."

"You, perhaps?" Sarcasm dripped from her lips. She pulled the door open wider. "I'd like the two of you to leave my pantry."

As if in slow motion, Derek bent down and scooped the maid's cap from the floor. "I'll tell you what, Patricia. Jess and I will not only leave the pantry, we'll leave.''

Patricia stumbled back, her owl-wide eyes staring from her ashen face. ''But Daddy's been looking for you.''

With Derek's prodding, Jess moved through the pantry doorway, dumbfounded, and picked up her shoulder bag.

''Tell your father I had an emergency.''

''But, Derek...'' Her tone heightened with authority. ''Don't you like working for Daddy?''

''I've enjoyed working for your father, Patricia. But not for you.''

He plopped the maid's cap on her head, turned to grasp Jess's arm and guided her toward the door.

Chapter Eleven

Sleep eluded Jess. Disbelieving last evening's events, she wrestled with her pillow throughout the night. Now she eyed the alarm clock—6:00 a.m. She sat upright and listened. The house lay in silence.

Rising, she inched back the shade and peeked out the bedroom window. A hint of frost lay on the grass, and a chill ran through her from the cold and her confusion.

But the icy thoughts melted with the warmth of her sweeter recollection. Like never before, Derek had displayed his allegiance and devotion. He'd dueled the enemy. His tender actions moved her.

For once Jess trusted him. He'd jeopardized his career, his anchor position, everything to defend her. He'd become her hero.

She slipped on sweatpants and matching shirt, then headed down the stairs. Her stomach rumbled with hunger. Though she'd prepared food all day yesterday, she hadn't had a moment to nibble one of the appetizers, and after the fiasco, she'd been too upset to eat.

She tiptoed down the stairs and past Derek's room. The door stood open an inch, and she retreated a step before seeing him, hands behind his head propped on pillows and staring into space.

His face looked tense, and she knew he was worried about his job. She had the same concern.

Tapping on the door frame, she opened the door halfway and waited.

His eyes shifted toward the sound. "Jess. Why are you up so early?"

"Same reason you are, I imagine. Thinking."

He beckoned her in.

She accepted the invitation, crossing the floor and sitting on the edge of his bed. "You're worried?"

He caressed her arm through the sweatshirt. "I suppose. I've given Holmes a few years of faithful service, and I'd hoped for…"

"A promotion. A future. It's what anyone would expect." Feeling the chill, she tucked her icy feet under the blanket folded at the foot of the bed and lay on her side with her head propped on her fist. "But you don't know for sure that the situation has changed."

"Not for a fact, but I can guess. Patricia isn't going to let my behavior go unnoticed by her father."

"Don't look for trouble," she said, distressed by the sadness in his eyes.

"I'll know soon enough. I figure as soon as I hit

the office this morning, Holmes will hand me my walking papers.''

She ran her hand along his exposed arm. ''Don't worry. Sometimes things have a way of working out for the best.''

''Sometimes they do, don't they? Like having you curled up on my bed.'' He smiled slyly. ''Come here,'' he said, urging her closer, the bedcover their buffer.

He eased his hand around her and rested it against her back, then drew her even closer. They lay together, face-to-face.

''We can't forget that one good thing came out of last night,'' Jess said.

''And what was that?'' he asked.

His gentle gaze melted her heart and left her breathless. Easing back, she ran a finger along his lips. ''You were my hero last night,'' she said. ''I've never had a man defend me like you did.''

His sadness faded and he chuckled. ''Have you needed defending?''

''That's beside the point,'' she said, using the lighter moment to shift her body and slide her feet to the floor. The temptation had grown too great. If she continued lying beside him, she would be asking for trouble.

He looked at her, sexy-eyed, enticing her back, but Jess stood her ground.

''Right now I need food,'' she said. ''I'm starving.''

''I'm hungry, too.'' With a mischievous look, he

reached for her and tugged her down beside him again.

"But I'm hungry for food." Playfully she pushed him away and stood. She crossed the room and paused by the door. "If you need me, I'm in the kitchen."

"I do need you, Jess." His groan followed her into the corridor.

"And I need food," she called back, forcing herself down the hall and into the kitchen.

Grateful that Meg was still sleeping, Jess headed for the coffeepot. Too many opinions, too many noses in the works, would only create more stress.

While Jess drank her coffee and ate toast slathered in butter, she heard doors opening and closing, then the bathroom shower, and finally Derek's footsteps in the hall. After she poured her second coffee, he came through the doorway.

Seeming preoccupied, he walked to the cabinet, grabbed a cup and poured coffee.

Hoping to distract him from his worries, Jess initiated a new topic from his morning concerns. "Time's flown. Friday's the big homecoming parade and game. Then the centennial dance is Saturday. Can you believe it? I've been here almost three weeks."

"Three weeks? It seems like a lifetime."

"Is that good or bad?"

Derek gave her a halfhearted grin. "I don't have to answer that, do I?"

She shook her head. "Did you remember the float decorating is tonight?"

"The what?"

"Meg asked us to help decorate one of the floats for the parade."

"That's the last thing I have on my mind." He set his mug on the table and lifted apologetic eyes. "I didn't mean to bite your head off, Jess."

"That's okay. I understand." If she had any brains, she wouldn't have asked. Why would he want to decorate a float when his career hung by a thin thread?

"Where will you be?"

"They're working at Delaney's Garage on Catalpa. When it's finished, they're parking it somewhere until Friday," she said, wondering why he'd asked.

"I'll be there eventually," he said. "Just make sure you wait for—"

The telephone rang. Derek's face paled. He eyed Jess with a look of resignation, then crossed the room and grabbed the receiver from the wall.

Wondering whether she should leave the room or stay, Jess's curiosity won out, and within a heartbeat, she knew who the caller was. Patricia.

"I agree," Derek said. "We both respect your father and want what's best for the station."

He eased the phone away from his ear, and Jess could hear the strident voice ripping through the receiver.

Bringing the phone back, he responded, "We need to talk, Patricia. No games this time. You have no real interest in me. In fact, I'm not even sure you like me. What you want is control."

He listened for a moment in silence.

"Can't this wait? I'll be in the office within the hour." He looked at Jess and shook his head.

But his expression changed, and Jess froze to the spot, sensing the worst.

"You want me to what?" His shoulders sagged, and he leaned against the wall, looking defeated, though his voice remained strong. "I'll pack up my desk, Patricia, but I'll do it when your father gives me notice. Last I heard he owned the station, not you."

He dropped the telephone on the hook. "I figured she'd at least wait until I hit the office."

Jess sat in the small study and faced the telephone. All morning her mind grappled with Derek's problems, while her heart ached. She'd caused the dissension more than anyone. If she hadn't walked into Derek's life, he'd have had his anchor job in a few months and she'd be in Cincinnati taking care of business.

Taking care of business. That was what concerned her at the moment. She watched the steam rise from her coffee mug with her hand resting on the telephone. With the other, she grabbed the hot coffee and took a sip. She needed to talk with Louise. Now.

Discussing the business face-to-face would be better, but Jess figured that being in Royal Oak, she could take advantage of the time and do some research. That is, if she knew for sure the partnership was about to end. End agreeably, she prayed.

She set the mug on the desk and punched in the numbers, relieved when she heard Louise's voice.

"Jess, you're back already. Thank God."

Jess winced at the harried sound in her partner's

voice. "I'm still in Michigan, Louise. Are there problems?"

"Only the usual. I was never meant to supervise the kitchen. I know you're against this, but I even ran an ad in the paper just to see who might show up for an interview. I've suggested so often we hire people to cook while we supervise, and I really think it's time. We have enough business now to let someone else run the kitchen. This isn't for me."

But it was for Jess, and she'd told Louise that too many times. "You don't like the hard work." Jess kept her I-told-you-so at bay.

"I had no idea how many hours you put into this place. Far more than I do."

Jess sank back against the chair, feeling more confident. "Glad you understand." She grabbed a quick breath and barreled forward. "I've been doing some serious thinking since I've been in Michigan."

"So have I." Louise chuckled. "You'd better get back before the holidays. We're booking fast."

Holidays. Jess lifted the mug and sipped the bracing coffee. "The holidays are getting close." Sadness ran through her. Thanksgiving and Christmas bookings usually excited her, but this year the thought of a busy catering season left her empty. She just wanted to be home.

But coming home to Royal Oak meant so many changes—and chances. How long would it take to build a business here? How much competition would she have? And how did Derek fit into her plans?

"I don't hear you, Jess. What's on your mind?" Louise asked.

"Since I got here, I realize how much I miss my hometown, Louise. I'm thinking I belong here."

Jess heard her partner's intake of breath. "You mean, leave Cincinnati?"

"Yes. I'd like to come back here and open a business. Add some of the features I've been talking about. You know."

"You're unhappy here?"

Jess sensed the rising tension. "It's not that I haven't enjoyed working with you, Louise. The partnership was what we both needed...then. But now I think going our own ways could be beneficial...to both of us. I've wanted to expand and you've wanted to hire workers and just supervise. We have different philosophies."

Silence weighed heavy on the line, and Jess closed her eyes, waiting for Louise to refuse to listen.

"To be honest, Jess, I've thought about this myself. I suppose you'd want me to buy your share of the business."

Jess swallowed her pride. If Louise didn't cooperate, her hope was gone. "That's the only way I could open a new place here. I don't have enough put away to keep myself above water and start a business."

"You certainly made this decision quickly," Louise said.

"Not really." A sinking feeling settled in Jess's chest and rested on her stomach. "It's been on my mind a long time."

Closing her eyes, Jess reviewed the details of a move. Not only selling her condo, but finding a house, a new shop, hiring help, new equipment. A big job, but one she felt driven to pursue.

And Derek? His face hung in her thoughts as brilliant as the moon in a summer-evening sky. Even if she avoided looking, he was there—bright and clear. Her heart dipped and rose like an ocean wave. The whole thing, the move and Derek, seemed unbelievable.

And what would she do if Louise said no?

Squinting into the morning sunlight, Derek parked his SUV and headed into the building. He'd made decisions and intended to stick to them. He stepped into the elevator, his heart in his throat.

Though he loved his work, hurting Jess as he had wasn't worth a job. Other stations in other cities hired experienced newsmen. He'd look elsewhere. Maybe in Cincinnati.

Jess's face haunted him—her hurt, humiliation, the damaged trust. Making up for what he'd done seemed impossible. Jess had given so much, and he'd given so little in return.

When the elevator doors slid open, Derek lifted his chin and strode down the hallway, trying to pretend nothing had happened. When he stepped into his office, he sank into his chair and took a deep breath.

What should he do first? Pack up his gear or face Holmes? He looked through the window and scanned his co-workers in the newsroom. Had they heard anything?

His door opened, and with the sound, his stomach

hit his shoes. The afternoon news anchor stepped through the doorway.

"Yo," Brian Lowery said.

A prickle of uncertainty sizzled up Derek's back. "What's up?"

"Not much. I wondered about the cocktail party." He sat in the chair beside the desk. "Successful?"

Derek gave him a long, slow look. Was Brian being subtle, or hadn't the fiasco reached his ears? "Things went pretty well," he said, thinking "pretty well" gave the truth some leeway.

"Glad to hear it. You worked hard on that project."

"It's not over. They're here for a couple more days." Derek dragged out his courage. "Heard any scuttlebutt?"

"Scuttlebutt?" Brian frowned. "I'm not sure what you mean."

Derek relaxed, deciding he might as well be honest. "Patricia and I had a little falling-out." He swallowed a disheartened chuckle. "More than a little."

"That's not hard to do. The woman's a control freak."

A faint grin tugged at Derek's mouth. "You can say that again. She fired me this morning."

"Fired you? You're kidding. She can't do that."

Derek shook his head.

"The woman needs a swift kick." Brian lifted his eyebrows and chuckled. "Now that you mention it, I haven't seen her today." Brian rose and headed for the door. "I wouldn't worry about it. No matter what she thinks, her daddy's the boss here."

Derek gave him a goodbye nod and wondered. He'd seen Holmes kowtow to his daughter too many times.

He eyed the stack of mail on his desk. He lifted the envelopes and flipped through them. Nothing that couldn't wait. He lifted the phone and checked his voice mail. Holmes's voice pierced his anxiety. His boss wanted to talk with him. Derek pushed the interoffice buttons.

Holmes's secretary came on the line. "I'll see if Mr. Holmes can talk now."

Waiting, Derek clutched the receiver.

The line came alive. "He can see you in his office now if it's convenient," the woman said.

Derek agreed and dropped the phone onto the cradle, slipped off his jacket and filled his quaking lungs before heading upstairs.

When he arrived, Holmes nodded to him from his desk and gestured toward a chair. "Come in. Have a seat."

Derek strode in and sank into the upholstery.

The large man studied him in silence. "You left the party early last night."

"I did. I'm sorry, but it was necessary."

Holmes gazed at some papers on his desk and ran his index finger around the edge of them. His severance papers, Derek assumed.

"I understand you and Patricia had a little problem."

Derek leaned forward, elbows on his knees, and folded his hands. Forcing his gaze from his shoes, he looked at Holmes. "More than a little problem, sir. A big one."

Chapter Twelve

As soon as Meg came through the doorway, Jess burst out with her news. "I'm moving back home, Meg. Coming back to Royal Oak for good." Saying the words lifted a weight from her shoulders,

Meg stopped dead in her tracks. "You're what?" She continued her journey into the living room and lowered herself into a chair.

"I talked with Louise. She agreed to buy my share of the partnership," Jess answered.

"You did this over the telephone?"

Jess laughed. "Naturally I have to go back and settle everything. But she's good for her word."

"Whew! You move like lightning, girl."

Filled with new energy, Jess rose and clutched her hands to her chest. "I am. I'm on fire. After Derek left for work this morning, I scanned the newspaper and made a few telephone calls. I might have found some property."

"Already? You're kidding."

"No, I'm not," Jess said, "I spoke with a woman who wants to sell her building. She owns a storefront kitchen where she makes candy. She seems to be disenchanted with the amount of work involved. She wants out."

Meg threw her head back and laughed. "She's disenchanted. What about you? Doesn't catering take a lot of time?"

"I've been catering for years. I'm used to it. Anyway, she'll sell me her equipment, too. And—"

Meg interrupted. "Drumroll, please." She lifted her hands and pretended to drum.

Jess grinned. "The price is great. It's exactly what I can handle."

Shifting from merriment to amazement, Meg gawked at her. "I had no idea you were even considering coming back for good."

"I've wanted a change, but I hadn't realized how homesick I was." She moved to the window and gazed outside. "Walking on these streets, seeing the old neighborhood, I don't know...everything felt right. Like Dorothy in the *Wizard of Oz*. 'There's no place like home.'"

Meg rose and stood beside her. "Has Derek been in on this?"

Jess shook her head. How could she share her excitement while his life appeared headed down the drain?

Resting her hand on Jess's shoulder, Meg looked into her face. "Has Derek asked you…"

"No. Not really," Jess said, anticipating the question. "Derek's part of the reason I feel good here…and seeing you again, but it's more than that."

Meg covered her face with her hands and walked away. "Guess what?" She stood still a moment before her arms dropped to her sides.

Jess focused on Meg's anxious face.

"Seems we'll be dealing with a long-distance friendship again."

Her comment sailed over Jess's head.

Meg sank into the chair again. "I'm about ready to move on. I've made some progress writing, but I feel…I don't know, I feel I need New York. Coming home gives me a breather, but that's about all I can handle." Her focus shifted to the floor. "My feet begin to twitch…"

Jess moved beside her and perched on the chair arm. "And your red shoes click together…"

Meg gazed at her, her eyes sparkling. "And I say there's no place like…New York."

"But you'll come back again. For a visit."

Meg nodded and put her arm around Jess's waist. "That's for sure. And especially when the people I love are here. So what do you do now?"

"I have to talk more with Louise." Filled with excitement, Jess rose and spread her arms outward. "She's willing to buy me out. She's already looking for help. Louise loves investing money, but she's not a chef."

"What will you do if the woman sells this place before Louise and you settle your affairs?"

"I think we can work things out without a hitch, and I have enough savings to make a down payment without Louise's payoff." Feeling more optimistic than she had in years, Jess wanted to dance around the room.

She twirled away and plopped onto the sofa. "Let's do something festive."

"Like decorate a float?" Meg asked.

"The float. I'd forgotten." She grinned. "I suppose that's festive."

Though Jess laughed, a thought nudged at her heart. She prayed Derek had a better day than he'd anticipated.

When he left the studio parking lot, Derek headed for Delaney's. Jess said she would be decorating floats, and checking his watch, he assumed she'd still be there.

When he reached the garage, though the street was lined with cars, one empty spot stood in front of the building as if it were waiting for him. Derek grinned at his good fortune, parked and headed across the pavement.

The flatbed truck stood alongside the garage, the structure too large for the doorway. Derek scanned the crowd. Though he chatted with people in passing, he was focused on finding Jess.

In a heartbeat her long, dark hair caught his attention; she was right in the thick of the workers. His empty stomach cartwheeled, and he muzzled his yearning to take her in his arms and tell her his news. But this wasn't the place. He'd save it for a private moment.

Jess looked up from her work and waved.

"Looks like you're nearly finished," he said, inspecting the colorful float that towered above him. Superman rose high in the center of a flatbed truck, his windswept cape and costume created with red, white and blue plastic flowers.

Her questioning eyes sought his.

"Later," he said, answering her silent question.

Though a look of disappointment settled on her face, she didn't push and changed the subject as she gestured to the papier-mâché Superman. "The float theme is folk heroes and super heroes." She took his hand and wove her fingers into his. "I wanted to build you up there."

Her eyes sparkled, and he longed to kiss her parted, full lips. "Thanks. But I don't deserve the honor. Superman's a real hero."

She raised on tiptoe and whispered, "You're much more real than Superman."

Joy rolled through his chest. He gave in to his yearning and slipped his arm around her waist. "Let's get out of here."

"There's still a little work to do," she said.

He eyed the flowered structure and motioned toward it. "Then let's get busy."

"Okay." Jess handed him a staple gun. "We can be out of here in no time."

He held the gun like a six-shooter. "Which dirty varmint should I lay low fer ya, ma'am?"

She chuckled. "How about attaching a few more flowers to the other side there?" She pointed to a sparse area to the left on the base.

He rounded the end of the float, and while Jess handed him the colorful plastic puffs, Derek stapled. In only a few minutes he stood back and scrutinized his job.

"Looks good," Jess said, offering him an immediate smile and picking up his Old West imitation. "That should do it, pardner." She gave a little bow and fluttered her lashes, her face as lovely and warm as a summer's day.

Jess's mood had brightened since he'd last talked with her, which aroused his curiosity. The stress he'd seen on her face the past few days had smoothed away, and her eyes had a fresh sparkle. He wondered what had lifted her spirit.

His mind flew back to the meeting with Holmes. Leaving his boss's office, Derek had felt more settled than he had in months. Today, he had a goal, a direction. He had enough of spinning his wheels in uncertainty.

With the float ready for storage, the crowd began to thin. Workers gathered their tools and equipment and made their way across the pavement.

Grabbing Jess's hand, Derek guided her toward the street, anxious to make their escape.

"Unbelievable." A voice bellowed behind them.

Together, they spun around to face the voice.

"Derek Randolph and Jess Cosette, hand in hand," the man continued. "What'll happen next?"

"Eat your heart out," Derek called back without stopping.

"Don't let anyone tell you miracles don't happen," Jess called over her shoulder.

No rebuttal came, and Derek squeezed Jess's hand, filled with a sense of completeness. She hadn't winced the way she did so often when people teased them about their relationship. Progress. It felt good.

At the SUV Derek paused. "Where did *you* park?" He narrowed his eyes and looked down the street at the scattered line of cars.

"I rode with Meg. She left already, but I figured you'd show up."

"I knew one day you'd trust me." Though he joked, Derek delighted at the change. He hit the remote and opened the passenger door. "How about some food?"

"Sounds good," Jess said, "but don't you want to talk first?" She climbed into the passenger seat, her gaze never leaving his.

"We can talk at the restaurant. I haven't eaten all day," he said, and closed the door.

When the chef lifted Jess's tangy concoction of beef, chicken and vegetables from the grill into a bowl, Derek dropped two dollar bills into the glass container.

One of the cooks let out a whoop, grabbed a rope

suspended above the huge grill and sent a resonant clang through the restaurant.

Jess collected the dish and made her way to the table. She set down her plate and sat. "I hate that bell. Tipping is one thing, but having the guy swing from that rope with that Tarzan yell is another thing. Everyone turns and gawks."

Derek patted her arm. "That's part of the fun— plus, it makes people who don't tip feel like jerks."

Fun? She didn't think so. When her spirits were high, Jess enjoyed the clang and the fun of choosing her stir-fry ingredients, but not tonight. Derek hadn't told her a thing, making her certain his situation was dire.

She'd tucked away her own wonderful news, not wanting to share it under the circumstances. How could she rejoice when he may have lost his job?

Jess spooned rice onto her plate and covered it with the meat-and-vegetable mixture. She lifted a forkful and took a bite. "Best stir-fry in town."

Derek focused on his own mixture of meat and spices. Pulling a tortilla from the warmer, he dished the mixture onto the flat bread, wound up the edges and sank his teeth into the roll-up. "Can't beat this."

He grinned, and though a look of pleasure covered his face, beneath it, Jess sensed anxiety. An anxious look meant he had bad news. If not, why hadn't he told her by now?

She speculated in every direction while attempting to swallow the food, but it clumped in her throat. Frustrated, Jess put down her fork, folded her arms and caught his attention. "Why are you keeping me in suspense?"

He eyed the tortilla, then set it on his plate. "Today's been crazy, Jess. I missed lunch, and I was starving." He lifted the napkin and wiped his mouth. "I knew if we started talking, we'd never stop. I figured I'd concentrate better on a full stomach."

"So is it good news or bad?"

His eyes softened, and a tender smile curved his lips. "It's good news. Great news."

Her fears scattered like excited birds. She leaned forward. "You mean you weren't fired? Patricia's threat meant nothing?"

"See, I knew you'd want to know everything. How can I eat and talk?"

"Talk with your mouth full. It's okay." She patted his hand like a mother giving her child permission.

He swallowed. "Holmes told Patricia she was too stressed out and suggested she take a trip to Europe. He's going to meet her in Paris in a couple of weeks."

"I wish someone would reprimand me like that," Jess said. "The woman's spoiled to the core."

"That's what Holmes said." Derek slid his hand over the table and touched hers. "He apologized for her behavior."

Jess reared back. "You're kidding."

"No. Quoting her father, 'Patricia's strong-willed and likes to tether people to her side.'"

"I told you he was a nice man."

Derek leaned back in his chair with a grin and

puffed out his chest. "I agree. He spent the next few minutes extolling my ability and charm."

"He's right. You have great ability."

Derek leaned closer. "What? No charm?" He sent her a devilish wink.

Jess's mood soared. "Your head's too big already."

Derek beckoned the waiter. "I'll get the check. Let's save the rest of this discussion for later."

Knowing everything was all right, she agreed. With her appetite, Jess wrapped a tortilla around the rest of her food, feeling no need to talk. Instead, she nipped off the end and savored the spicy seasoning.

When they were finished, Derek slipped his wallet from his back pocket and pulled out the cash, then dropped the money on the table. "We can go if you're ready."

"More than ready," Jess said.

He rose and pulled back her chair as she stood. Jess slipped on her sweater and followed him around the tables. When she stepped outside, a brisk breeze whipped at her clothing. She shivered.

"Is Meg home?" Derek asked, slinging his arm around her shoulders and nestling her body against his side.

"I don't think so. One of her old boyfriends invited her to dinner. She told me not to wait up."

"Then we can go home. I hate to say it, but I'd rather talk with you alone," Derek said.

His comment left Jess thoughtful. They walked the

short distance to the car in silence. Jess climbed inside, still riddled with questions.

When they entered the house, Derek paused in the kitchen. "How about a soda or, better yet, wine."

"Wine? Are we celebrating?"

"Could be." He pulled an uncorked bottle from the refrigerator and grasped two fluted glasses from the cabinet.

"What do you mean?" Jess asked, following him into the living room.

He set the glasses on the coffee table and poured. Jess sank into the chair.

"Here's the good news," Derek said, handing Jess a filled goblet. "Since Holmes is going to Europe in a couple of weeks, he's cranked up his schedule for the news-anchor interviews."

"When?" she asked, accepting the drink.

"Friday." He sat on the sofa across from her and took a sip of wine.

"This Friday?"

He lowered his glass and nodded.

"That's wonderful, Derek."

"Don't get too happy. Friday's a couple of days away. Who knows what will happen? He's meeting with my competition tomorrow, and Holmes said he'd be out of town Thursday."

"After all you've done for the station, I can't imagine that he'd pass you by."

"We'll see. I just don't trust what I hear. Listening to him talk, it sounds like I'm a shoo-in but—"

"Shoo-in? Then we must have convinced him you're almost a married man."

"I'm not sure about that." He winked. "Anyway, I'm not getting my hopes up." He lifted his glass, rolled the deep-red liquid around and took a slow sip.

The marriage idea fluttered through Jess's heart. For years she'd given up on love and marriage. She'd been too busy and disillusioned. So many men she'd known had proved to be empty shells, looking for a moment of fun or a wild fling. Flings and one-night stands weren't her style. Derek hadn't asked for a one-night stand or a fling. He'd expected nothing.

Derek looked relaxed and hopeful. Gazing at him, Jess marveled at what the past weeks had brought. A new career for him. A new home and business for her. And what else? She could only dream. Who would have thought that the big, boorish teenager would turn out to be a talented, handsome gentleman who made her feel contented and loved?

Jess sipped the smooth merlot and decided it was time to tell him her surprise. "Are you ready for my news?"

His gaze sharpened with curiosity. "News?"

Toying with him, she only nodded.

A frown skittered across his face. "You're not going back to Cincinnati already?"

"No...I'm moving back to Michigan."

His body was propelled forward. "Moving back?" He searched her face. "You're not kidding me, are you?"

"Would I kid you?" She grinned.

In a heartbeat he reached her chair and knelt in front of her.

Jess put her palm against his cheek. "I'm selling Louise my share of the business and opening a catering shop here. I hope you'll give me a good reference...."

"Reference? I'll give you more than that." He stood, grasped her hands and drew her up into his arms. As natural as morning, their lips met, warm and intense. Jess threaded her fingers through his herb-scented hair, basking in his strong, protective arms.

When she eased back slightly, Derek's gaze held her captive. "Tell me more. I want details."

Wrapped in his arms, she told him the gist of all that had happened. He listened, enrapt.

"Just like the business," he said, "it's a fresh beginning...in so many ways."

"Yes. Fresh beginnings."

"For our careers," he added, "and for us." He paused. "But this time you and I start at the fifty-yard line. Even score. No fancy plays. Just steady movement forward...toward our goal."

Jess shook her head. Football. Though the man had left the game, the game had never left the man. "And what is our goal?" She held her breath.

"Love."

She wanted to hear him say the words. "Love life? Love animals?"

"Each other," he said. "We're a touchdown, Jess. You and me."

Hidden beneath his silly analogy was what she

wanted to hear. Like a magnet, her gaze locked with his. Her heart succumbed to the pull of his as inevitably as the tide responds to the pull of the moon. Her future seemed as brilliant as the sun on a July day.

Clear, bright and beautiful.

Chapter Thirteen

Jess helped Meg clear the dinner dishes. She'd been preoccupied, wondering what kept Derek. He usually called when he would be late, but tonight...nothing.

Not wanting to worry her friend, Jess kept her thoughts to herself. Struck by a more optimistic thought, she wondered if Holmes had arrived back early and conducted the interview for the news-anchor position this evening, instead of tomorrow.

But her optimism drifted, and concern marched back into her thoughts. Logic told her the interview would happen tomorrow as planned. So why didn't Derek call to say he'd be late? What had distracted him? A different fear slithered down her spine. An accident?

Jess eyed the clock. "I think I'll snap on the TV." She rose and walked toward the doorway.

"I'll be there in a minute," Meg said, putting away the last of the leftovers.

In the living room, Jess headed for the remote and punched in Channel 5. The news had already begun, and her chest tightened while she waited.

With one feature story completed, the camera focused on the news anchor. "A fiery crash ended a life on I-94," the newsman said. A video began to roll— the freeway, fire trucks, ambulance, police cars.

Jess strained her eyes, trying to identify the make of the charred vehicle. Was it an SUV? Tears filled her eyes when the camera pulled back and Derek looked at the viewers. "One life was tragically lost this evening on a Detroit highway. I'm Derek Randolph, overlooking…"

The words faded and only Derek's serious face aimed at the camera filled her thoughts. An accident, yes, but not *his* accident. Instead, a story he was covering.

"So that's where he is," Meg said as she dropped into a chair. "He missed a good lasagna."

Finally able to smile, Jess shook her head. "He won't miss anything. It'll be his midnight snack."

Focusing again on the news story, Jess's mind drifted to a fresh awareness. The idea surprised her. Though Derek would gain prestige as a news anchor, had he considered what he would lose?

Jess had listened to his voice, watched his excitement as he related the stories he covered. Derek stood on the spot, covering each tragedy or victory as it unfolded. Burning buildings, fiery crashes, daring rescues—he gathered the facts and shared them with viewers.

Excusing herself, Meg left the room, and Jess shifted to the recliner. She pulled the lever and leaned back, her mind whirring with questions and concerns.

The flash of headlights through the window snagged her attention, and Jess leaned forward and righted the chair.

In moments Derek's footsteps thudded in the kitchen. She rose and headed for the kitchen to warm his dinner and give him food for thought, as well.

The next day, while the cameramen coiled the cords and packed away the equipment, Derek jotted notes on a pad and climbed into the Channel 5 van. He eyed his watch, waiting with apprehension. The filming had taken longer than he expected, and being late for his interview with Holmes was the last thing he wanted to do.

"Almost ready?" he asked through the window.

"Another minute," his co-worker yelled back.

Leaning his head against the headrest, Derek listened to the clang and thud of equipment being stowed in the back. Today the familiar sound set him on edge. Anticipating the interview with Holmes, Derek supposed. So much depended on it.

Facing a new realization, he rubbed his neck. Was he deluding himself? What was really rankling him? He'd never been irritated by the cameramen loading equipment. He loved the sound, because it meant he'd covered a story. He'd been at the center of action. He'd lived a drama.

Being a reporter meant more to Derek than presenting a news story to viewers. It meant being part of people's lives at the moment the situation occurred. He cared about people, about their well-being, their joys and sorrows.

Jess's comments niggled in his mind. Last night while he ate, she'd questioned him. Probed. Challenged. She reminded him of his love for on-the-spot news. Standing in front of the camera with life going on around him...not in a studio behind a desk, but amid the flames, the laughter, the smiles, the tears. Today her words settled in his brain like a dart. She'd hit the truth. Bull's-eye.

"Ready," the driver said, swinging into the seat and starting the engine. "I know you have an interview."

Struggling with his thoughts, Derek only nodded and stared into the muted afternoon sun—not yellow, but a milky white shrouded by an autumn haze.

He thought of the parade crowd. Folks waiting on the curb to hear the bands and see the floats, to celebrate Royal Oak High School's one hundredth year.

In a couple of hours he'd promised to meet Jess at the parade. During the taping, he'd felt a brisk wind coming from the north and tugging at the burnished leaves. He would have to grab a heavier coat before he met Jess. But before that, the interview. Derek checked his watch again.

The van sped along the freeway, then took the ramp

to the surface streets. Derek knew he'd be on time, but instead of relaxing, he felt his shoulders tighten and knots form at the back of his neck.

As he rubbed the tension from his neck, Derek's seasoned ears caught the sound of a distant siren. Then two sirens. He'd learned to recognize them—police and emergency medical service. A third siren screamed as the noise intensified, coming nearer.

"Looks serious," the cameraman said from behind him.

Distressed, Derek watched a police car, EMS vehicle and a fire truck turn two streets ahead of them. He looked upward and saw smoke curling into the sky. Residential. A house fire.

"It's your call, Derek," Jerry Drummond said from the steering wheel. "What do you want to do?"

Jess and Meg shouldered their way through the crowd gathered on Main Street. Restaurants along the main drag had been filled with diners looking out from their tables along the windows, waiting to elbow their way into the crowd outside when they saw the first float.

The brisk autumn air sent a shiver down Jess's back, and she looked at the clouded sky, longing for the sun. Jiggling in place to keep herself warm, Jess heard the thud of a bass drum echo against the buildings. Everyone in the crowd leaned forward, craning their necks.

Instead of looking toward the music, Jess checked over her shoulder. Where was Derek? She assumed his interview had ended an hour ago. She'd told him where she'd be in the crowd.

Perhaps the interview had gone badly. Maybe Holmes broke the news he'd chosen the other reporter for the new position. What would Derek do? Would he meet her here or head home...depressed?

Meg stood near the curb, a wide grin on her face, and not wanting to darken her mood, Jess kept her worries to herself and forced her attention to the parade. Local bands, old jalopies, floats, bicycles and wannabe clowns made their way along the street, pausing occasionally, then marching along again.

Cheers rose as the people gathered along the curb spotted friends or a special float. When Superman rolled past, she and Meg laughed and cheered like high-school kids.

"Not a bad job for amateurs," Jess said, trying to capture the spirit of the celebration. She waved at people she knew who followed the float dressed in plastic Superman costumes.

"I wonder what's keeping Derek," Meg asked after the float had passed. "I thought he'd be here by now."

"Me, too," Jess said, harnessing her concern.

"What time was his interview?"

Although she'd checked her watch only minutes earlier, Jess checked again. "At one, I think. It's after three now."

Without the sun's warmth, a damp chill clung to the late-afternoon air. As the crowd drifted away, a crisp breeze whipped at Jess's jacket and sent an icy sensation through her. Or was it her distress?

"I wonder if he's with the crew covering the parade," Jess asked, grasping for a logical explanation.

"I don't know," Meg said, tugging her coat more snugly around her. "But it's freezing. Let's walk that way and see."

The parade had already passed by the time they reached the camera crew. Jess stood back for a moment watching them rolling cables and stowing equipment. No one looked familiar. At last, she stepped forward and asked, "Has Derek Randolph been around?"

"Not around here," a man said, his attention on his work.

"I thought maybe he'd been asked to cover..." She shook her head. "Never mind. Thanks, anyway"

The man nodded, and she turned to Meg. "What do you think?"

"Let's find our car."

Not knowing what else to do, Jess agreed and followed her.

Meg unlocked the doors, and Jess climbed inside, grateful to be out of the wind.

"Are you going to the football game?" Meg asked as they pulled away. "It's homecoming."

"No, I'm not a football fan. I'd rather go home, if you don't mind."

"Are you sure? Derek may show up at the game."

Jess shook her head. "No, he specifically said he'd meet me at the parade." She hugged herself for warmth. "I'm chilled, anyway. This jacket just isn't enough."

"I have gear in the back. Flannel blankets and padded cushions for the football bleachers."

"No. Just home."

"That's fine. I'm meeting some friends at the game, so I won't be alone."

While Meg chattered about her friends and the house party to follow, Jess struggled with her worries. The rainy evening that Derek had stormed into her life seemed eons ago. In three short weeks, her world had changed and would never be the same again.

Meg pulled into the driveway and Jess hopped out, removing the house key she used during her stay from her bag. She waved goodbye, then headed for the door, disappointed that Derek's car wasn't parked in the driveway.

Something was wrong, she felt it.

She twisted the key in the lock and stepped inside. The lonely house hummed with silence. Jess headed for the kitchen, draped her jacket over a chair back and put on the kettle for tea. She longed for something hot and brisk to warm her.

While the water heated, she walked into the office and checked the answering machine. The red light blinked. Her heart leaped. A message.

Although uncomfortable listening to someone else's messages, Jess hit the button, hoping to hear Derek's voice with an explanation.

She sat on the desk chair and propped her chin in

her hand, listening to the computer-generated voice. "You have one new message. Friday, 5:04."

"Hello, Derek. This is Donald Thompson from NBN in New York. I know this is sudden, but we would like to talk with you as soon as possible. I think we have a job offer you can't refuse. If you call the network tomorrow and I'm not in, I've given my staff instructions to give you my private number. I'm anxious to talk with you." The telephone disconnected.

"End of messages," the computer voice announced.

Jess stared at the machine, tears pushing against the back of her eyes. Just as her life had gathered hopeful momentum, she found herself sliding into a dark pit of uncertainty.

Had Derek already heard the message and forgotten to erase it? Had he flown to New York tonight to negotiate a deal with NBN? She rose and hurried back to the kitchen. Maybe he'd left her a note.

Jess scanned the counters. Nothing.

She ran to the living room. Nothing.

The kettle whistled from the kitchen.

After pulling out a teabag and mug, Jess poured water into the cup and settled at the table. What if Derek hadn't been home? Maybe he hadn't heard the message. Jess wanted the decision to be Derek's. His alone. With no interference from her. Meg was returning to New York. Derek would be in New York. Perfect…

For them.

A car door slammed, and Jess heard a sound at the

door. If it was Derek, she'd resolved to say nothing about the message.

"Jess," Derek called from the front hall. "I'm so sorry." He strode into the kitchen and came to a halt. "I know I'm late—is something else wrong? You look like you lost your best friend."

The truth of his words struck her heart. The irony tugged a laugh from her chest. "Just cold. We nearly froze at the parade."

He slid into a chair beside her. "The tea smells good. Orange and spices?"

She nodded.

"It is nippy out there." He placed his icy hand over hers.

"Would you like a cup? The water's hot." She rose without waiting for an answer and occupied herself with the tea, struggling to compose her flailing emotions. "I was a little worried about you," she said, keeping her back to him.

"I figured you would be, Jess. I'm sorry." His voice softened and she heard him draw a deep breath. "When we were heading back to the studio for my interview, we ran into a major story. We were the first ones on the scene."

Interview? Story? Confused, she turned to face him.

Stress pulled at his face. His eyes looked glazed, his mouth tense.

"What happened?"

"A house fire. Tragic. A mother and child trapped in a second-story bedroom. Two children escaped.

Horrible. I've been interviewing neighbors...and the father when he arrived home.'' Derek's voice broke with emotion.

She saw the sorrow in his face and said, "Awful. I don't know how you interview people when it's so real and—"

"It's my job. It's what I love to do." The words sailed from him like a revelation. "I missed the interview, Jess. It's for the best. You were right, you know."

Multiple thoughts tumbled from his lips while Jess became tangled in his words, struggling with the paradox of joy and sadness. NBN wanted Derek. Her own reaction lay tied to her tongue. Should she say I told you so? Should she say I'm glad you realized what was best suited to you before it was too late? She remained silent.

"I've shocked you," he said, grasping her hand and drawing her to his side. He patted his knee and she lowered herself onto his lap, her head tucked against his sport coat, her tears hidden from view. "Everything will be fine, Jess. Now we can concentrate on you and me. Nothing to interfere with making each other happy."

She nodded against his cheek, swallowing the sobs that tore at her throat and the truth she knew in the answering machine.

She took a deep breath, pulled herself from his shoulders and looked into his eyes.

Derek cupped her cheeks. "I love you, Jess. I love you with all my heart."

"You love me?" She'd yearned to hear him say those wonderful words, and now they slid through her like satin ribbon and wrapped sadly around her heart. "I've tried not to...but I can't deny it anymore. I love you, too, Derek."

His lips touched hers for only a moment. The gentle pressure sent an electric tingle through her body. Drawing back, she gazed into his face, so filled with love.

At her heartfelt sigh, he frowned and tilted his head in silent question. Derek in New York, she thought. Her business in Royal Oak. But no matter what happened, Jess knew this was where she wanted to be.

Unbidden, courage nipped at her conscience. If she truly loved Derek, he deserved to know that happiness awaited him with only the push of a button. New York...

"Derek."

"What's wrong?"

She shook her head. "Nothing's wrong. It's wonderful. Check your answering machine." She slid from his knee.

He rose, curiosity spreading across his face. "Wonderful?"

She nodded.

He darted through the doorway while loneliness shivered through her body. She covered her face with her hands.

Once touched by love, Jess realized loneliness had a whole new meaning.

Chapter Fourteen

In the quiet, sleep-filled morning, Derek sat trance-like with his hand still clutching the telephone. He'd spoken with Thompson and couldn't believe his good fortune. While the New York VIPs had looked at their plans for syndication, they had also watched him. He had no idea they'd been keeping their eye on him for the past year, viewing his special reports and news stories.

A new world spread out before him. He'd sell the old house, say goodbye to his hometown and head for the Big Apple, the city that had tantalized his sister for years.

He'd heard Meg complain about traffic and expensive parking, but for a man who liked to be in the thick of things, New York was the place to be.

Monday, he'd fly to the studio, review the financial package he'd heard on the telephone and make his decision. But in truth, the decision had been made the moment he'd called Donald Thompson.

He credited it all to Jess. She'd sent a nugget of thought working through his brain. Did he really want to be an anchor—or did he want to do what he loved? Jess, the woman he loved...

But now what? Jess had decided to move back to Royal Oak, a hometown where he'd been until today. And now he...

Footsteps sounded on the stairs, and Derek swiveled around in his chair and waited. Jess appeared in the hall, dressed in jeans and a T-shirt, her dark hair hanging over her shoulders. The most beautiful woman he'd ever seen.

Sleepy-eyed, she looked through the doorway and paused. "Did you call?"

He nodded. "It's an amazing offer, Jess. Great benefits, great salary, and I'd be a special reporter on a new show called Life-Line. They'll do unique specials on all kinds of compelling people and dramatic situations. The sort of reporting I love."

She leaned against the doorjamb, a pleasant smile on her face. But Derek knew her too well. The smile covered something deeper...something cheerless. "I know it's a shock, Jess."

Stepping forward, Jess rested her hand on the edge of the desk. "No, Derek. It's wonderful. Perfect. How could I not be thrilled for you?"

He rose and caught her hand, wrapping his fingers around hers. "But what about us?"

"Us?" A sad smile flickered on her lips now.

"We've had an autumn romance. It's been wonderful, but…like we said the other night, we both have fresh beginnings. You in New York and me in Royal Oak."

"No, Jess, please. I know this relationship has swept us like wildfire. Three weeks ago you were Frenchie, my sister's string-bean friend, and I was Derek, the fat kid who bungled along and fell into a great career. But now, today, we love each other. A job offer can't change that. Not the feelings."

"Love is funny. It comes and goes. One day I love grilled cheese. The next day I'm tired of it. One day—"

Anger boiled up Derek's chest. He pulled his hand away and his back stiffened with frustration. "You comparing our feelings to a cheese sandwich?"

"I didn't mean—"

"You mean more to me than diamonds, never mind cheese—no matter how it tastes in one of your hors d'oeuvres. Our relationship means more than cheese or television cameras…or careers."

"Derek, please."

Tears glazed her eyes, and he drew her into his arms, feeling her soft breasts heaving with her gasps.

"Let's not be rash," Derek said, running his fingers over her silken hair. "Let's think this through carefully. We have options. We have choices."

He felt her head move in a slow, thoughtful nod.

Saturday evening, Jess, Meg and Derek entered the high school. The place was festooned with school sweaters from eons past, pennants, posters garnered from old yearbooks and other memorabilia. Crowds gathered in front of the bulletin boards and displays, talking about old times. Adding to the spirit, Royal Oak had won the homecoming football game, and now alumni, students and residents joined in the double celebration of the annual homecoming and the school's centennial.

Despite her confusion, Jess decided to attend the dance as if nothing had happened. Derek's forlorn face had provided motivation, as well as her determination to be a true friend. While her heart ached, her brain cheered Derek's new opportunity.

As she'd planned earlier, Jess wore the amber-colored sheath of shimmering silk that Meg had so admired the day she bought it.

Standing beside her, handsome in a three-piece, navy pin-striped suit, Derek radiated charm as he spoke with old and new friends. Earlier in the day, he'd been quiet. Thoughtful. And Meg? She was gorgeous as usual.

Her own thoughts spiraling, Jess breathed in the heady scent of his aftershave. She loved so many things about him that her thoughts were weighted with sadness. When she looked his way, his eyes spoke volumes, but she saw no solution to their dilemma.

Friends came and went, chattering and laughing about the game and sharing tidbits of the past ten years.

As the evening wore on, Derek grew quiet again. Jess studied him, wondering where his thoughts were leading him. Yet the look in his eyes told her everything would be all right.

"We need to talk, Jess," he said finally.

"Here?" She looked at the milling crowd.

He motioned toward the door. "Let's walk," he said. He grasped her arm, and she followed.

In the cafeteria a few small tables sat against a back wall, all occupied. Derek shrugged and, instead, guided her down an empty hall. They halted by a folding metal gate that closed off the rest of the building.

Wrapped in silence except for the distant music, Jess leaned against the grating, afraid to look into his eyes.

Derek's hand captured hers and he brought it to his lips.

The soft touch took her breath away.

"I've made a decision," Derek said. "As I mentioned yesterday, we have options and choices. I've made mine." The set of his chin looked bold, and confidence filled his eyes.

The expression addled her. "What do you mean? You haven't met with them yet. You're not going to New York until Monday."

"I don't need to meet with them. I'm staying here…to be with you."

"Oh, no, you're not. Not when this is the job of a lifetime." She pulled away. But blocked by the metal grating, she didn't go far. "You're going to New York, and you'll be wonderful and successful."

"I'm not going without you."

The words pinned her to the spot more securely than the grating. New York? She jostled the impinging thought from her mind. "We both have too many decisions to make. I have a business to sell and an apartment to rent. I'll be back in Cincinnati for weeks while you're getting settled in New York. You'll be with Meg and—"

His mouth captured hers and ended the litany she'd spouted to cover the emotion that vaulted through her. She could not fight her yearning, and her mouth accepted his, the tongue that teased and sent her pulse rate roaring. Meanwhile her mind flashed like neon. Derek belonged in New York. Where did she belong?

His gaze filled with feeling, Derek eased back. "I'm staying here, Jess."

"No, you're not." The answer came like a bolt of lightning. "You can't. Who'll I spend my nights with when I'm in New York and you're here?"

Derek looked stunned, confused. Then his eyes cleared and a hesitant grin flickered across his face. "When you're in New York?"

She nodded. "The more I think about it, what difference does it make if I start a new business here or there? It's a fresh beginning either place. And in New York, I know a successful author and a big-name newsman who'll give me wonderful references." Remembering his response days earlier, she added, "He'll give me more than references, I'm sure."

"You can say that again." His smile faded, and his gaze locked with hers. "Are you sure, Jess?"

"Positive."

To her delight, Derek knelt on the floor and clasped her hands in his. "If you're positive, Miss Cosette, I'd like to make you Mrs. Randolph. Will you make me the happiest man in the world and be my wife?"

"This time we're not pretending?" she asked. But looking into his eyes, she didn't need an answer. "I will marry you any time, any place."

As if on cue, a familiar love song drifted down the empty corridor. Derek nestled Jess into his arms, his cheek resting against her hair while they swayed to the soft, pulsating rhythm.

"I love you, Jessamy Cosette."

Jess nestled closer against his broad, familiar chest. "I love you, Derek Randolph, with all my heart."

Wrapped in the music, Derek slid his hand beneath her chin and lifted her face to his. Their mouths met, soft and eager...the kiss she knew he'd waited a lifetime to share. Like two melting candles, their bodies molded into one. Warm, soft and new.

* * * * *

SILHOUETTE *Romance*™

Lost siblings, secret worlds, tender seduction—live the fantasy in...

A TALE OF THE SEA

Separated and hidden since childhood, Phoebe, Kai, Saegar and Thalassa must reunite in order to safeguard their underwater kingdom. But who will protect *them*...?

July 2002
MORE THAN MEETS THE EYE
by Carla Cassidy (SR #1602)

August 2002
IN DEEP WATERS
by Melissa McClone (SR #1608)

September 2002
CAUGHT BY SURPRISE
by Sandra Paul (SR #1614)

October 2002
FOR THE TAKING
by Lilian Darcy (SR #1620)

Look for these titles wherever Silhouette books are sold!

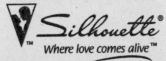

Silhouette®
Where love comes alive™

Visit Silhouette at www.eHarlequin.com   SRTOS

If you enjoyed what you just read,
then we've got an offer you can't resist!

Take 2 bestselling
love stories FREE!

Plus get a FREE surprise gift!

Clip this page and mail it to Silhouette Reader Service™

IN U.S.A.
3010 Walden Ave.
P.O. Box 1867
Buffalo, N.Y. 14240-1867

IN CANADA
P.O. Box 609
Fort Erie, Ontario
L2A 5X3

YES! Please send me 2 free Silhouette Romance® novels and my free
surprise gift. After receiving them, if I don't wish to receive anymore, I can
return the shipping statement marked cancel. If I don't cancel, I will receive 6
brand-new novels every month, before they're available in stores! In the U.S.A.,
bill me at the bargain price of $3.34 plus 25¢ shipping and handling per book
and applicable sales tax, if any*. In Canada, bill me at the bargain price of $3.80
plus 25¢ shipping and handling per book and applicable taxes**. That's the
complete price and a savings of at least 10% off the cover prices—what a great
deal! I understand that accepting the 2 free books and gift places me under no
obligation ever to buy any books. I can always return a shipment and cancel at
any time. Even if I never buy another book from Silhouette, the 2 free books and
gift are mine to keep forever.

215 SDN DNUM
315 SDN DNUN

Name	(PLEASE PRINT)	
Address	Apt.#	
City	State/Prov.	Zip/Postal Code

* Terms and prices subject to change without notice. Sales tax applicable in N.Y.
** Canadian residents will be charged applicable provincial taxes and GST.
   All orders subject to approval. Offer limited to one per household and not valid to
   current Silhouette Romance® subscribers.
® are registered trademarks of Harlequin Books S.A., used under license.

SROM02   ©1998 Harlequin Enterprises Limited

eHARLEQUIN.com

| community | membership |
| buy books | authors | online reads | magazine | learn to write |

Visit eHarlequin.com to discover your one-stop
shop for romance:

buy books

❦ Choose from an extensive selection of Harlequin,
   Silhouette, MIRA and Steeple Hill books.

❦ Enjoy top Silhouette authors and *New York Times*
   bestselling authors in Other Romances: Nora Roberts,
   Jayne Ann Krentz, Danielle Steel and more!

❦ Check out our deal-of-the-week specially discounted
   books at up to 30% off!

❦ Save in our Bargain Outlet: hard-to-find books at great
   prices! Get 35% off your favorite books!

❦ Take advantage of our low-cost flat-rate shipping
   on all the books you want.

❦ Learn how to get FREE Internet-exclusive books.

❦ In our Authors area find the currently available titles of
   all the best writers.

❦ Get a sneak peek at the great reads for the next
   three months.

❦ Post your personal book recommendation online!

❦ Keep up with all your favorite miniseries.

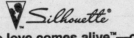

Silhouette®

where love comes alive™—online...

Visit us at
www.eHarlequin.com

SINTBB